SOME FRIEND . . .

"I did it," Ali shouted, waving the envelope. "Look, Tess! Twenty-five dollars! We're going to have the greatest time at the carnival."

Tess's face was bright red with anger. "You cheated! You never built that bike yourself, Alison Hinkle."

Ali flushed. "I—I did most of it," she stammered. "My family just helped me with the hard parts."

"Your family!" Tess shouted. "They do everything for you! They even win contests for you."

Alison fought her hardest not to lose control. "Come on, Tess," she said. "What does it matter which of us won?"

"It matters to me!" Tess shouted. "Because I tried my hardest, and I did it all myself. Nobody helped me."

"You're just jealous," Ali called as Tess started to wheel her bike away. "You can't stand it when anyone is better than you."

Tess turned back. "You can keep your dumb family," she yelled. "I never want to see any of you again."

Don't miss these exciting books from HarperPaperbacks!

FRESHMAN DORM
by Linda A. Cooney

#1 *Freshman Dorm*
#2 *Freshman Lies*
#3 *Freshman Guys*
#4 *Freshman Nights*
#5 *Freshman Dreams*
#6 *Freshman Games*
#7 *Freshman Loves*
#8 *Freshman Secrets*
#9 *Freshman Schemes*

THREE OF A KIND
by Marilyn Kaye

#1 *With Friends Like These, Who Needs Enemies?*
#2 *Home's a Nice Place to Visit, But I Wouldn't Want to Live There*
#3 *Will the Real Becka Morgan Please Stand Up?*
#4 *Two's Company, Four's a Crowd*
#5 *Cat Morgan, Working Girl*

Coming soon:

Janet Quin-Harkin's **FRIENDS** #2:
  Tess & Ali and the Teeny Bikini

FRIENDS

Starring Tess & Ali

JANET QUIN-HARKIN

HarperPaperbacks
A Division of HarperCollins*Publishers*

This is a work of fiction. The characters, incidents, and dialogues are products of the author's imagination and are not to be construed as real. Any resemblance to actual events or persons, living or dead, is entirely coincidental.

HarperPaperbacks *A Division of* HarperCollins*Publishers*
10 East 53rd Street, New York, N.Y. 10022

Copyright © 1991 by Daniel Weiss Associates, Inc.
and Janet Quin-Harkin
Cover art copyright © 1991 by Daniel Weiss Associates, Inc.

All rights reserved. No part of this book may be used or reproduced in any manner whatsoever without written permission of the publisher, except in the case of brief quotations embodied in critical articles and reviews. For information address Daniel Weiss Associates, Inc. 33 West 17th Street, New York, New York 10011.

Produced by Daniel Weiss Associates, Inc.
33 West 17th Street, New York, New York 10011.

First printing: May, 1991

Printed in the United States of America

HarperPaperbacks and colophon are trademarks of HarperCollins*Publishers*

10 9 8 7 6 5 4 3 2 1

Chapter 1

Hi, Keri!
You are so lucky you're going to Disneyworld this summer.

Alison Hinkle leaned back in her beach chair and chewed on the end of her pen. On either side of her stretched a wide expanse of golden sand. The ocean sparkled and glittered just beyond her toes. It was a perfect day for swimming or a trip to the water-slide park. If only she had someone to go with her. She looked up and down the beach. A few feet away, her seven-year-old brother Robbie was busy building a city in the sand. A couple of toddlers splashed at the edge of the water, squealing when waves came to meet them. A few grown-ups dotted the sand, lying under colorful umbrellas, reading or sleeping.

The postcard Alison was writing showed a scene of Rose Bay, the resort town a mile down the road. In the picture, the beach was crowded with people swimming and playing volleyball. It

1

looked like a fantastic place to spend the summer. Everything happened in Rose Bay. Nothing happened on the quiet stretch of private beach where Alison was lying. Last year she had been allowed to ride her bike into Rose Bay with Mandy Johnson. Mandy wasn't her best friend—she whined and liked to have her own way—but she could be fun sometimes. Mandy wasn't coming this summer, and Alison was only allowed to go to Rose Bay if she went with her older brother, Josh.

Her mother didn't understand how humiliating it was to tag along behind her brother! He wasn't crazy about having his little sister with him either. When he met his friends at the pool or the public beach, he'd either ignore Alison or embarrass her in some way.

Alison sighed and started to write again:

I guess Melina's at camp by now and Renee's in Bermuda. I'm the only one not doing something exciting this summer. It's so boring here, I don't know how I'll survive until September. Mandy Johnson isn't even coming this year. Sometimes it seems like there's no one else my age on the whole island. I'm going to go crazy! My Mom's being a pain—as usual. She won't even let me ride my bike into Rose Bay alone—in broad daylight!

If I haven't died of boredom by the time you get back, maybe you can come spend a few days with me.

Love, Ali

Alison slipped the postcard into the book she had been reading and began to apply another layer of sunscreen. With her fair hair and freckles, she had to be careful or she'd burn.

If that happens, Mom will probably make me stay in the house for the rest of the summer, she thought.

Not that she wasn't used to her mother's rules by now. She had always been the only one not allowed on sleepovers at houses where her mother didn't know the parents, the only one not allowed to stay out past nine-thirty or go to movies rated PG-13. But enough was enough. Somehow she had to make her family see that a person who was almost twelve and starting junior high was not a baby anymore.

But Alison had no idea how to change things. To her family she was still Little Alligator, the nickname her mother had called her since she was two weeks old. She had a horrible premonition that she'd still be Little Alligator when she was ready for college.

Alison put down the bottle of suntan lotion. Her back was sticky with sweat. She got up and walked down to the edge of the water, feeling the wonderful coolness creep up from her toes. The ocean was smooth as glass beyond the waves, which broke with a gentle hiss. She longed to run out and dive in, but she wasn't allowed to swim by herself. She looked hopefully in the direction of her grandparents' house. There was no one in sight.

Alison shielded her eyes against the sun, looking back at the big wooden house, which rose above the dunes. Grandpa had built it as a summer home back when his children were small—three stories of weathered gray wood with gabled attics at the front and back. *If only Grandpa had built a condo in Florida, I could be at Disneyworld with Keri right now,* she thought. She had really wanted to do something different this summer.

"Keri's going to Epcot," she had said casually to her mother. "Why don't we ever do stuff like that?"

"Because we always spend our summers at the beach," her mother had answered smoothly. "Your grandparents would be disappointed if we didn't come."

"We could go to Florida," Alison had said hopefully, "and still have time to come here."

Her mother had shaken her head and smiled.

"Maybe one year, when Robbie's old enough," she had said.

Alison got the feeling that her mother would always come up with an excuse because she liked coming to Rose Bay. The rest of the family liked it, too. Josh never seemed short of friends to hang out with at the public beach or the swimming pool. Robbie was content to sit by himself for hours at the edge of the water, building cities in the sand.

Alison looked across the vacant lot toward the Johnsons' white cottage. She remembered peeking out of the upstairs window with Mandy the summer before, watching the waves crash against the shore after a storm.

Just then she noticed a big orange truck in the Johnsons' driveway.

"The Johnsons have come after all," she yelled to Robbie. "I'm going over to see if Mandy's there."

She broke into an excited run, scrambling up the dunes toward the Johnsons'.

The moving van was parked in the sandy lane behind the house. Two men were wheeling a huge object down the ramp. It was wrapped in cloth, but Alison guessed from its shape that it was a piano. A man came out of the house, running toward the truck, waving his arms wildly. He was tall and skinny, with a beard and lots of dark hair that flopped into his face as he ran. "Gently with that," he yelled. "Take it slowly."

Alison stopped in midstride, her mouth open in surprise. It was not the Johnsons at all. She had never seen this man before in her life.

Chapter 2

Alison darted behind the hedge as a woman came out of the house. She had long black hair that hung down around her face and a flowing dress with loose sleeves. She was young and pretty, but very pale. "Max, leave them alone," she called after the man. "I'm sure they know what they're doing."

"It's my piano, Maggie. I don't want anything to happen to it!" the man snapped, and went on helping to steer the piano along the pathway to the front door.

"I thought we agreed you'd cut back on work this summer," the woman said. "You do have a family as well as a piano, or hadn't you noticed?"

Alison lingered for a moment, then decided to creep back the way she had come, hugging the hedge in case she was seen. She really wasn't interested in meeting these people. As Alison crept along, she heard a girl's voice on the other side of the hedge.

"Hup, Rajah! Rajah, jump . . . good lion! Good lion!"

Alison stopped in her tracks. Very cautiously she crept closer and found a spot where the sea winds had eaten away at the greenery. She crouched down and peered through the hedge.

What she saw made her burst into laughter. A girl was kneeling on the grass between two upturned boxes. Alison could not see her face, just a lot of dark hair falling over her shoulders. Sitting on one of the boxes, facing a hoop, was not a lion at all, but a brown lop-eared rabbit.

The girl looked up when she heard Alison's giggle, and their eyes met through the hole in the hedge. The girl had a thin, intelligent-looking face with big dark eyes that somehow seemed too large for the rest of her. Alison felt challenged by her gaze.

"That's not a lion," she said. "It's a rabbit."

The girl brought her finger up to her lips. "Shhh!" she warned. "He doesn't know that. I've brought him up to think he's a lion."

"Why?" Alison asked.

"I'm practicing for when I get one," she said, as if this was the only logical answer. "Rajah's all I've got right now, and he's not very easy to train. I figure after him lions will be easy."

For a moment Alison considered saying nothing and disappearing quickly. Then she realized that although this girl was strange, at least she was not boring! And she did seem to be about the same age as Ali.

"I live next door," she said. "Can I come in?"

"Of course," the girl said.

Alison got up and pushed open the little white gate. The girl sat back on the grass and took the rabbit onto her lap, idly stroking his ears.

"I'm Tess," she said. "What's your name?"

Alison came and sat beside her. "Alison," she said. "Alison Hinkle."

Tess grinned. "Do you want to be called Alison Hinkle?"

"Well, my friends call me Ali."

"Ali sounds much better," Tess agreed.

She looked at Ali as though she were taking in every detail. Ali was suddenly conscious of her freckles and her peeling nose. "Are you here for the summer?" Ali asked.

"No, Max always brings the moving van for a weekend," Tess said, then laughed at Alison's serious face. "Just kidding. What grade are you in?"

"Going into seventh."

Tess's face lit up for the first time. "Me too!" she said.

"Are you really planning to train lions?" Ali asked.

Tess nodded. "When I join the circus."

Everything began to make sense to Alison. Tess's family was a circus family—that's why they all looked and behaved so strangely. "I see," she said. "You're all in a circus."

Tess looked around. "Who?"

"Your family."

"My family's not in a circus," Tess said, horrified.

"I—I thought you just said you were going to join a circus," Alison stammered, wishing she had not started the conversation after all.

"I am," Tess answered. "What's wrong with that?"

Alison shrugged. "Nothing. Only, you have to admit it's not the sort of thing ordinary people do."

"Then I guess I'm not ordinary," Tess said. "I've always wanted to join a circus—since I was three years old."

"Wow," Alison said, impressed. "And your parents are going to let you?"

Tess shook her head. "I plan to run away and join one as soon as I get an act together. Maybe by the end of junior high."

"Wow," Alison said. "A lion-taming act?"

"Training," Tess corrected. "You can't tame lions. They always remain wild beasts. I've read all the books," she said. "Now all I need is a real lion to practice on. . . ."

She put the rabbit onto the grass and rolled over onto her stomach. "I realize that in a crummy apartment in New York City there wouldn't be any room, but I thought if we came out here for the summer one lion wouldn't be too much to ask for." She made it sound very reasonable. Alison couldn't tell if she was kidding or not. "But I never get what I want," she said with a sigh. "What sort of pets do you have?"

"None," Alison said. "There are five people in my house. My mother says that's plenty of work without animals. They let Josh have a mouse once, as a sort of trial run on pets, but it died."

"Josh?"

"My brother. He's fourteen. He's going into high school this year."

"Wow, you have a brother. You're so lucky."

Alison made a face. "You wouldn't think I was so lucky if you had to share a bathroom and a phone with him," she said. "I have a younger brother, too—Robbie. He's going into second grade."

Tess turned over and threw herself onto her back, spreading her arms wide so that the rabbit leaped away in alarm. "Imagine . . . two brothers! That's why you need that great big house next door."

Ali grinned. "My grandparents live there, too,

and sometimes other aunts and cousins come to visit."

Tess's eyes opened wide. "You have grandparents, too? You *are* lucky!"

"Don't you have grandparents?" Alison asked, astonished.

"There's only Maggie and Max and me," Tess said sadly, ruffling Rajah's ears as she spoke. "My grandparents all died before I was old enough to remember them. That wasn't very nice of them, was it?"

Alison shook her head, thinking that Tess's grandparents probably hadn't died by choice.

"But I suppose I'm lucky to have had two parents this long. Most people don't these days, do they?" Tess went on.

Alison considered this. "I guess not," she said.

Tess sighed. "Nobody in our building is married anymore. At least, not to the same person they started out with." She got to her feet suddenly, sweeping Rajah up by the scruff of his neck. "Want to see my room?" she asked. "We unloaded that first."

Alison jumped up. "Sure," she said. "But just for a minute. I have to get back for tea."

"Tea?"

"Uh-huh." Alison made a face. "My grandmother likes the whole family to sit down to tea every afternoon."

Tess looked amused. "Really?"

Alison nodded. "My family is kind of old-fashioned. We have a lot of traditions, like coming out here every summer and having tea and supper together every day."

"I didn't think families like that existed anymore, except on TV," Tess said.

Alison laughed. "Yeah, well, we're probably the only one," she said. "I wish we weren't sometimes. It can be a pain."

"How come? It sounds like fun."

"Not when it's your turn to clean up from dinner. There are lots of rules, and there's always someone older to decide what to watch on TV," she said.

"But at least there's always someone to talk to," Tess said. "I'd like that. Max and Maggie hardly ever talk."

"Max and Maggie?"

"My parents."

"You call them by their first names?"

"Sure. They like me to," Tess said. "Come on, let's go up to my room." She lifted the rabbit up to her face and kissed his nose. "I have to put Rajah away first," Tess said. "Max is allergic to animal hair." She scooped Rajah under one arm and skipped toward the house. Alison admired the way she moved, as if there were springs in her legs. Alison felt she could never skip like that.

She took after Grandpa Hinkle, and was solidly built with a round face and sandy hair that turned strawberry blond in the summer. Tess stopped and looked back. "What?" she asked.

"Nothing. I'm coming," Alison said, hurrying to catch up with Tess.

Chapter 3

"Here, hold Rajah while I open his cage," Tess said, thrusting the rabbit into Ali's arms. Ali took him awkwardly, feeling the unfamiliar warmth and softness.

"I hope he'll be okay out here," Tess said, putting him into the cage. "I really want to build him a bigger house."

She shut the door, kissed the rabbit through the bars, then began to walk away. "It's a miracle that you showed up," she said. "I was all set to lie on my bed and sulk all summer. I really didn't want to come here."

"Why not?" Ali asked.

Tess shook her head, and her heavy dark hair swayed from side to side. "It was Maggie's dumb idea," she said. "Max and I are city people. It was Maggie who thought that maybe . . ."

She broke off suddenly then went on in a different sort of voice. "I mean, Maggie likes painting oceans, and there sure is a lot of ocean here." Ali watched her, wondering what had made Tess

15

change like that, almost as if she was playing a part.

"I'd love to see my mother's face if I called her Helen," Ali said, trying to get back to normal conversation. "She'd probably have a heart attack."

She thought this would make Tess laugh, but Tess seemed far away.

Ali was dying to ask Tess what was wrong. She sensed that Tess was trying hard to hide how upset she was. But she didn't want to seem too curious to someone she'd known for only five minutes. Instead she asked, "Is Tess short for something? I never heard that name before."

"It's short for Contessa," Tess said. "That's countess in Italian. Maggie and Max were staying with a countess in Italy when I was conceived. That's when they decided to get married."

"Oh," Alison said, looking down at her feet. Tess didn't seem at all embarrassed. She opened the French doors at the back of the house and turned back to Ali.

"Come on in," she said.

She led the way into the big living room, which Ali remembered had always been full of heavy old furniture. Now it contained a piano and some pillows.

Alison stopped to look. "What happened to the furniture?"

"The Johnsons' furniture?" Tess asked. "That's all stored in the room at the front."

"But when is yours coming?" Alison asked. "Didn't the van bring it?"

"This is ours," Tess said. "Maggie doesn't like a lot of clutter. Of course, she hasn't put up her artwork yet. She has to see how the sun shines in before she decides which things go on which walls." She looked around in obvious satisfaction. "Come on," she said. "My room's upstairs."

There was no sign of Tess's parents. Alison followed Tess up the stairs and into the bedroom that used to be Mandy's. The room now had only a mattress on the floor, and it was practically hidden under a huge pile of stuffed animals. There were two huge bears, a long boa constrictor, several penguins, a whale, and a couple of dinosaurs.

"Wow," she said. "You've got a lot of animals."

"Max and Maggie won't let me have any real ones, besides Rajah," Tess explained, "so I have to make do with these." She reached down and lifted a brontosaurus by the neck. "When I was little I really wanted a pet brontosaurus. Didn't you?" she asked.

"Uh, no," Alison said. It had never crossed her mind to want a pet brontosaurus. "I bet your parents wouldn't get you one of them either."

Tess nodded. "I wish dinosaurs still existed.

Just think what neat pets they'd make. I used to imagine how I'd ride mine to school and tie him up to the bike rack to wait for me."

"He'd cost a lot to feed," Alison said.

Tess giggled. "You're not kidding."

"And you'd need a whole separate house to store his dino-chow," Alison added.

"Dino-chow?" Tess laughed. "Think of the commercials on TV: Dino-chow is Dinomite! Give it to your bronto, pronto!"

She beamed at Alison.

"Boy, am I glad I met you," Tess said. She flopped down on the mattress among the animals and cleared a space for Ali beside her. "I thought everybody here would be over the age of sixty-five and I'd go crazy."

Ali sat down carefully. "I hate to tell you this, but most people *are* over sixty-five. Everyone except my brothers and me and my Mom."

"Are your parents divorced?" Tess asked.

"No," Alison said. "My dad has to work during the week. He drives down on weekends and usually comes for the last two weeks of August."

Tess stood up and walked across the room to the window, resting her elbows on the ledge. "Is there anything to do around here?" she asked, looking out at the deserted beach.

"Well," Ali said, coming to join her. "There's a pool and a public beach not too far away, but you need a car to get to the boardwalk and the movie theater. They're over the bridge in Southhaven. There is one great thing that happens here. There's a gigantic carnival in August."

"Yippee! I love carnivals," Tess said. "Does it have rides?"

"Awesome rides," Alison said. "There's a parade and a barbecue and fireworks."

As she spoke, a wonderful picture formed in her mind: she and Tess together, going up in the Ferris wheel, clinging to each other as they were flung around in the Tilt-a-Whirl and screaming together in the haunted house. . . .

"I'll finally be able to go on the scary rides!" Alison exclaimed. Tess gave her a questioning look.

"I never had anyone to go on with before," Ali explained. "My big brother always went off with his friends, and my little brother only likes the lame kiddy rides. Mandy Johnson, my only friend here, always had to go home before the carnival. But this year, we'll go together."

Tess paused as if she'd just remembered something, then she tossed back her hair. "I sure hope we stick around that long," she said.

"Don't you think you will?" Alison asked worriedly. It looked as if she had miraculously found a friend for the summer, and she didn't want that friend to disappear.

Tess shrugged her shoulders. "Who knows?" she asked. "It's hard to tell right now with Max and Maggie." She turned to the window so that Alison couldn't see her face. Then she turned back with a smile. "I'll make them stay. I'm not missing out on the chance to go to a carnival."

Ali felt sorry for Tess, even though she was not sure why. Again she had the sense that something was upsetting her new friend.

"Which city do you live in?" she asked.

"New York," Tess answered. "What about you?"

"Outside of Philadelphia," Alison said. "A very ordinary suburb."

"So what's there to do until the carnival arrives?" Tess asked. "Other than swim and sunbathe?"

Ali shrugged her shoulders. "There's miniature golf down past Rose Bay. And there's a waterslide park on the way to Southhaven. They're both fun, but I hardly ever get to go because I'm not allowed to ride my bike that far."

"How far is it?" Tess asked.

"A couple of miles."

"That's not far."

Alison looked down. "I know, but my mother doesn't like me riding my bike there alone."

"How come?" Tess asked. "There isn't too much traffic around here, is there?"

Alison studied her toes. "It's not the traffic. It's just the way she is. She thinks I'm helpless."

"Wow. She really does sound old-fashioned. I'm allowed to go anywhere I want," Tess said proudly.

"Anywhere?"

Tess thought for a moment. "Well, maybe not some places, like the subway at midnight, but anywhere reasonable. I've been riding the bus to school since I was eight."

"You're lucky," Alison said.

"Oh, sure," Tess said. "Believe me, riding the bus alone when you're eight years old isn't that great. So what's the public beach like?"

Alison got the feeling Tess was changing the subject again. She wondered why Tess had boasted about her independence and then was so quick to put it down. *She doesn't realize how lucky she is*, Alison thought. *I'd give anything to be able to ride the bus to the mall with my friends or even to ride my bike without getting permission.* She realized that Tess was looking at her, waiting for an answer.

"The beach is nice," she said, "but on weekends and the Fourth of July it's wall-to-wall bodies. It's worth going though, just to see the cute lifeguards. . . ."

Tess grinned. "Why are lifeguards always

cute?" she asked. "Do you think they have to pass a cuteness test?"

"Maybe," Ali said, laughing. "There were a couple of real hunks there last year. But my favorite place in Rose Bay is a little store that makes the greatest saltwater taffy. . . ."

"What's that?"

"You've never had saltwater taffy?" Ali asked. Tess shook her head. "Does it taste salty?"

"No, it's candy. It's made of this real sticky stuff that gets pulled and stretched on a machine in the window. It almost breaks your jaw when you chew it, but it tastes great."

"Yum! I can't wait to try it," Tess said. "Maggie doesn't like me to eat too much candy, because of my teeth."

"Just like my mom," Alison agreed.

"Parents are a pain, aren't they?" Tess asked.

As if on cue, the sound of raised voices came up from the garden below.

"If you're going to be so childish about it! . . ." the man's voice shouted.

"Me? Childish? I only asked . . . ," the woman's voice demanded. "Oh, forget it." Then a door slammed, making the whole house shudder.

Ali gave Tess a nervous glance. Tess shrugged her shoulders. "They're not getting along too well at the moment. You know how parents are," she said.

Alison's parents never screamed at each other or slammed doors, but she nodded as if she agreed. "I'd better be getting home," she said. "I'll get in trouble if I'm late for tea."

"Can I come back with you and meet your family?" Tess asked.

Alison bit her lip. "It might not be the best time right now," she said. "Today's a horseshoe day."

"A what?"

"We always play horseshoes with Grandpa on Thursdays," Alison said.

"Honestly?" Tess asked.

"I swear," Alison said with an embarrassed giggle. She wasn't about to admit it, but she sort of liked playing horseshoes with her family. They all cheered and teased one another and tried to beat Grandpa, but never did. "It sounds weird, doesn't it? That's the way my family is. Everything has to be just the same every summer."

"So why can't I come when you're playing horseshoes?"

"I guess you could." Alison hesitated. "But it might not be the best time. My grandpa likes to win, and he might say you'd ruined his concentration. He has kind of a bad temper."

"Okay," Tess said. "What about after horseshoes?"

"I don't know. We usually play until dark. . . ."

"So I'll come by when you've finished."

"Would your parents let you come over after dark?" Alison asked. "There are no street lamps out here."

"Are you kidding?" Tess asked. "It's only next door."

Alison tried to remember a time when she had been allowed out alone after dark. "What time do you have to be in bed?" she asked.

"When I'm tired," Tess said. "We don't exactly keep regular hours in our house. Of course, during the school year they make me go to school, so I have to get up in the mornings. But during vacation . . ." Her voice trailed off as someone started playing the piano very loudly.

Tess raised her eyes. "If he goes more than three hours without playing, he gets withdrawal symptoms," she said.

"Your dad?"

Tess nodded.

"Is he a piano player?"

"A pianist," Tess said in a fake haughty voice. "Actually a composer. He writes songs. Have you heard of *That Summer*?"

"Which summer?" Alison asked. Tess laughed.

"It's the name of a musical, dummy," she said. "My dad wrote the music. He's working on a new one now. At least, he's going to see whether he can write when he's not in the city." She frowned down at her animals for a second, then looked up brightly again. "I wonder if Maggie's unpacked any food yet. I'm starving."

"And I have to get home," Alison said.

"So I'll fix myself lunch while you have tea."

"It's almost four o'clock," Alison said. "Is that when you usually eat lunch?"

"I eat when I'm hungry," she said.

She led the way back down the stairs. Tess's father did not look up, and Tess did not try to introduce Alison. Tess's mother was in the kitchen, staring out the window. She jumped when Tess spoke to her.

"Oh, Tess, there you are," she said. "There is still a mountain of boxes waiting to be brought in, including most of the food." She noticed Alison for the first time. "Oh, I didn't know you had a friend with you."

"This is Alison from next door," Tess said. "This is Maggie."

"Hi, Alison," Maggie said.

"Hi," Alison mumbled, not able to call a grown-up by her first name.

Maggie looked around. "I can't offer you anything to eat or drink, I'm afraid. . . ."

"It's okay," Alison said. "I have to get back anyway."

25

"She has to be home for tea," Tess said. "She has grandparents, and they sit around a tea table and play horseshoes."

"Not at the same time," Alison said, and they all laughed.

"Isn't there a great view from this window," Maggie said, gazing out again. "I wonder which box my watercolors are in."

Tess made a face to Alison. "That means I'd better bring the food in before it all rots," she said. "Once she finds her watercolors, she won't think of anything else."

Maggie didn't even turn around when Alison said good-bye.

"So should I come over tonight?" Tess asked.

Alison was dying to have Tess over. But her family was strict and old-fashioned and had probably never met an eleven-year-old girl who went to bed when she was tired and ate when she was hungry and called her parents by their first names. It was important to her that they like Tess, and she knew that her mother wouldn't like the idea of an eleven-year-old wandering around in the dark. "You'd better wait till morning," she said. "Grandpa goes to bed really early."

"I get the feeling you don't want me to meet them."

"I do," Alison said. "It's just that they have this strict routine and they hate anything that breaks into it, so it's important that you arrive at the right moment. I really want them to like you, because we've got a whole summer ahead of us and it will be such fun. . . ."

"It's okay. I understand," Tess said. "I can't wait to meet them and see if they're as weird as you say."

"They're not weird," Ali said.

"Okay. Not weird. Interesting, different," Tess said. "What time should I come over in the morning?"

"We have breakfast around eight," Alison said.

"That early?" Tess looked horrified. Then she said, "Okay. I'll be over right after breakfast. Then maybe we can eat saltwater taffy and break our jaws. Okay?"

Alison nodded happily. "Sure. See you tomorrow."

She smiled as she crossed the driveway and headed for her house. Tess wasn't like any girl Ali had ever met before, certainly not like her friends at school. *But it doesn't matter,* Alison thought. *I've got what I wanted—someone to do things with all summer long.* She opened the front gate and ran all the way home, her legs feeling as light and springy as Tess's.

Chapter 4

Tess showed up the next morning just as Alison's family was finishing breakfast.

Robbie was the first to notice Tess's face peeking in the window.

"There's someone spying on us," he said.

Alison looked up. "It's Tess," she said excitedly as she jumped up.

"Sit down and finish your breakfast, Alison," her mother said. "I'll get the door."

Alison waited, her sausage poised on her fork, wondering what her mother would think of Tess. She had tried to be careful about what she told her family about Tess the night before, especially what she told her mother. Alison's mother had taken an instant dislike to some of the girls at school because they were rumored to be "wild." Alison didn't want her mother to get any wrong ideas about Tess.

"Her family's really interesting," she had mentioned when they were all watching Grandpa throw the perfect horseshoe. "Her father's a composer and her mother's an artist. Isn't that interesting?"

Alison's mom was very big on culture. She dragged Ali and Josh to the symphony at least four times a year. Ali saw her mother's eyes light up. "A composer? That is interesting," she said. "The little girl is probably very musical." She gave Ali a knowing look. "And I bet she never has to be forced to practice the piano. . . ."

Ali was sure Tess was not forced to do anything, but she was glad her mother already saw Tess as a "good influence." She held her breath now as her mother opened the door, hoping Tess wouldn't blow it.

Before Mrs. Hinkle could say anything, Tess swept in. "Hi, you must be Alison's mom," she said. "You look just like her. I was going to wait until later to come over, but then Maggie started painting and . . ." She broke off when she spotted Daisy, Grandma's old spaniel, who came out of her usual trance and noticed a stranger had come into the room. Daisy didn't like strangers. She usually interrupted her nap to growl and bark at them.

"What a sweet dog!" Tess exclaimed. She knelt in front of Daisy. "Come here, sweetie pie. Come here, you cute little honeybun."

Daisy had even been known to bite strangers. "Watch out, she sometimes . . . ," Grandma began, but before she could finish, Daisy had broken into a very spirited waddle toward Tess, her little tail wagging crazily. With a sigh of bliss she collapsed on the floor and rolled onto her back so Tess could rub her tummy.

Everyone stared in amazement. Daisy was never friendly to strangers.

"She's obviously taken a fancy to you," Grandma said, sounding surprised and pleased.

"All animals like me," Tess said. "That's because I love them. I plan to work in a circus."

"A circus?" Ali's mother asked.

"Hey, Ali, you didn't tell us that," Josh said, giving her a dig in the side. He grinned at Tess. "I thought she'd already told us everything there was to know about you. She's talked about you nonstop since she got home."

"Shut up, Josh," Ali said.

"Well, Alison," Grandpa said in his deep, stern voice. "Aren't you going to introduce us to your friend?"

Alison flushed. "Sure, Grandpa," she said. "Everyone, this is Tess. Tess, this is my family . . . Grandpa, Grandma, Mom you've met, and these two are Josh and Robbie."

"Hi," Josh and Robbie mumbled. Tess beamed at the boys. "Hi," she said. "Alison told me all about you."

"Probably nothing good," Josh said.

30

"No way. I told Ali how lucky she is to have brothers. It's so boring having nobody to fight with."

"See, Al," Josh said, smiling at Robbie, "we are good for something. You just never appreciated us before. Right, Rob?"

"Uh-huh," Robbie echoed. "We're having breakfast right now," he went on. "You want some? My grandma's a good cooker."

Everyone laughed, and Grandpa said, "That's right, Grace, aren't you going to offer the poor girl something to eat? She looks like she needs fattening up to me."

"Come and sit here, Tess," Grandma said, springing into action. "Can you make room beside you, Robbie? Josh, go get an extra chair. Can I cook you a sausage or some bacon, dear?"

Tess's big, dark eyes opened even wider. "Sausage and bacon? Wow!"

"Is something wrong?" Grandma asked.

"It's just that . . . sausage and bacon . . . all that cholesterol . . . We never . . . I mean Maggie never buys . . ."

"Poppycock," Grandpa roared, fiercely enough to make Alison jump in her seat. "All this nonsense about cholesterol. Poppycock, I say. Look at me, young lady," he said to Tess. "Do I look healthy?"

"Sure," Tess said, grinning up at him. She

didn't appear the least bit scared by his booming voice.

"Of course I'm healthy. My doctor says I have the body of a fifty-year-old man, and I'll be seventy-six this fall!"

"Okay," Tess said. "I'll take some of that sausage and bacon. I want to look like Grandpa when I'm seventy-six."

"You've got a smart friend, Alison!" Grandpa said, laughing. He drained his coffee and went out. Grandma put a big plate of sausage and bacon in front of Tess, who attacked it as if it were the first food she had seen in months.

Alison's mother sat on the stool beside Tess. "We're so glad Alison's found a new friend. She's been so lonely this summer," she said. "She always had Mandy Johnson next door in the house you're staying in. But the Johnsons couldn't come this year, and Alison was afraid she'd have no one to play with."

Alison shot her mother a withering look. "Mom, I'm almost twelve. We don't play anymore."

Her mother gave Grandma an amused look. "Well, whatever you do together, then . . . hang out?"

"See what I have to put up with, Tess?" Alison muttered as Tess finished the last bite of sausage.

"More sausage, Tess?" Grandma asked. "You look like you enjoyed the first one."

"Well, maybe just one more," Tess said. "This cholesterol doesn't taste half bad!"

Grandpa reappeared in the doorway, a battered old hat perched on his head.

"Well, I'm off fishing," he said. "Work up good appetites for lunch. I might bring home a whale!"

"A whole whale?" Robbie asked.

"Grandpa's just teasing, honey," Ali's mother said. "He couldn't catch a whale."

"Besides, they're an endangered species. There's an international ban on whaling," Tess said.

"What do you want to do today?" Alison asked quickly. She could tell that her family liked Tess so far. She didn't want her to blow it by saying anything that her family would think of as weird.

"Let's go fishing with your grandpa," Tess said, jumping up from the table. "I've never been fishing before."

Alison's mouth opened, but no sound came out. Grandpa's fishing expeditions were private and sacred. He never took anyone with him. Sometimes he would take the children down to the jetty and show them how to fish, but never on one of his real expeditions. But Tess was already dancing over to his side. "Can we come with you?" she asked. "I'd love to try fishing."

Five pairs of eyes focused on Grandpa, waiting for him to explode. Instead he said, "Sure, why not. Come on, if you're coming. Fish won't bite when it gets warm later."

"Come on, Ali," Tess called. "You heard what Grandpa said!"

Alison got to her feet hesitantly. Grandpa handed them each pieces of his equipment to carry.

Ali took the tackle box he gave her. She was beginning to believe that Tess was not an ordinary girl at all, but some sort of magical being. What else could explain the way her family had immediately accepted her? *Maybe some of Tess's magic will rub off*, Alison thought, *and I'll be allowed to do what I like, the way she does!*

Her dreams of freedom were interrupted as her mother grabbed her at the front door. "Don't forget the sunscreen, honey," she said, waving an open bottle. "Here, let me put it on you before you go out."

"Oh, Mom," Alison said, embarrassed. "I can put on my own sunscreen, you know." She took the bottle before her mother could get the lid off.

"Well, make sure you do," her mother said. "I don't want my Little Alligator to burn." She ruffled Alison's hair.

"Bye," Alison said quickly.

Tess gave her an amused look as they shut the front door. "Little Alligator?" she asked.

Alison's face flushed. "She always calls me that. It's so embarrassing. Doesn't your family have any strange nicknames for you?"

"None," Tess said. "Max and Maggie have always treated me like another adult. They never spoke baby talk to me or any of that stuff."

"I wish my family would treat me like an adult," Alison said with a big sigh. "In fact, I wouldn't even mind if they'd treat me as if I was almost twelve."

"Tell them that's how you want to be treated," Tess said as if the answer was totally simple.

"It's not as easy as that," Ali said. "I try everything with my mother. I've tried arguing. I've tried pleading. She just smiles and pats me on the head and calls me Little Alligator!"

"Come along," Grandpa boomed, striding out in the direction of the beach. "Fish won't bite if it gets too hot."

They set off behind him.

Tess looked at Alison, and they both started to giggle. Grandpa turned around. "I'm not taking any gigglers with me," he said. "It will disturb the fish. Understand?"

"Yes, Grandpa," the girls said in unison, struggling to keep their faces straight.

Chapter 5

The three of them made their way along a narrow sandy path to Grandpa's favorite fishing spot.

"Wow, this is nice," Tess said, looking at the broad sweep of sand and the fishing boats bobbing at the rickety wooden wharf in Rose Bay. "It's just like a postcard, isn't it? I guess that's why Maggie chose it."

Alison had spent so many summers in Rose Bay that she had stopped noticing how pretty it was. Now she had to agree that it was very special. It had none of the things that spoiled so many other resorts along the shore—no flashy signs or tacky souvenir stalls.

She felt pleased and proud of it now, as if it was *her* place. "Yeah, it is pretty nice," she said modestly. "There's the public beach . . . and see the pool? You can just see the high dive sticking up," Alison instructed. "My brother hangs out there all the time."

"Careful with my rods," Grandpa growled,

turning back to them as the path petered out and the rocks began.

They exchanged a look and followed him out onto the rocks, stepping carefully as the dry rocks became more slippery. Finally, Grandpa set down his basket and net on a high, safe place. "I'm going to fish out here," he said. "Alison, take your friend back a bit and show her how to bait up a hook. You know as well as I do, if you've paid attention all these years."

He turned to Tess. "I used to bring Alison fishing in her playpen and give her a little line to hold."

"Really?" Tess asked.

"He's just teasing," Alison said.

"You don't remember?" Grandpa asked, his eyes twinkling. "Once you caught a huge fish. You would have been jerked right into the ocean, but the bars of your playpen saved you. You didn't let go of the line, though, just like I'd taught you."

"Oh, Grandpa, don't say things like that," Alison said, blushing with pleasure because the story made her sound like a hero. "Tess will believe you!"

"She should believe me—it's true," he said. "Here, take some bait and get going."

"Come on, Tess," Alison said. "I'll show you."

Tess was already hopping, nimble as a goat,

over the slippery rocks. "How about up here?" she called, scrambling up to where a sharp rock jutted out over the ocean's edge. "You get a great view from up here. Hey, Ali, look. I'm the Statue of Liberty!"

"You can't cast from out there," Ali said. "The line will get caught in the undertow." She led the way back to a low, flat rock. "This will be good," she said. "The water's nice and deep here." She squatted down among the warm, dry seaweed and began to undo the line on one of the rods.

Tess squatted down beside Alison. "The water here's really beautiful," she said. "I don't think I've ever seen an ocean as clear as this."

Alison peered into the water. "Yes, it's really clear today," she said. "We went snorkeling once, right off these rocks, and we saw a giant octopus."

"No kidding?" Tess said, her eyes glowing with excitement. "I've got to learn to swim this summer. I've never had the chance. With the sort of life Max and Maggie lead, we never seem to make time to go to a beach."

"You said your father wrote a musical. Is he famous?" Alison asked.

"I suppose so," Tess said. "Although composers aren't famous like rock stars. Nobody ever stops him in the street or anything. Maggie's well known as an artist, too," she added.

"Wow," Alison said. "Two famous parents. So do famous people come to your house all the time?"

Tess trailed one hand in the water. "I've met lots of famous people."

"Rock stars?"

"Yeah, I've met some rock stars," Tess said. "My dad's thinking of writing a musical for Del Lindsay."

"Del Lindsay?" Alison yelled. "He's one of my favorites. Have you met him?"

"Not yet," Tess said, "but I'm sure I will."

"I can't believe it," Alison said. "I am sitting here with a girl who knows rock stars. Wait till I tell Renee and Melina in the fall."

"Who are they?"

"My friends in school," Alison said. "You are so lucky."

"Right," Tess said sharply. "I'm just *sooo* lucky." She pushed her long hair behind her shoulders. Then she frowned out to sea for an instant before jumping up. "Are you going to show me how to bait a hook or not?"

Alison nodded, wondering what had made Tess so angry. She got out the plastic bag. "You take a mealworm like this . . ."

"A what?" Tess asked.

"They're called mealworms."

Tess peered into the bag. "They're still alive."

"Of course. Most fish don't like dead worms."

"You want me to put a live worm on a hook?"

"It's not hard."

"But it's cruel."

"Worms don't feel anything," Alison said.

"You're sure?"

"Yes."

"You do it," Tess said, stepping back. "I couldn't."

"Okay," Alison said. "You just get the worm and slip it on like this." She demonstrated, feeling very brave. Usually she hated this part so much that she had Grandpa do it for her, but with Tess watching she felt like an expert fisherwoman. "There," she said, careful not to let Tess see her shudder. "Now, I'll show you how to cast."

She took the rod and jerked it outward. The line curved in an arc and the hook landed way out in the smooth, deep water. Alison thought she had done a pretty good job of casting.

"Okay, what do we do now?" Tess asked, obviously not noticing.

"You want to try?" Ali asked.

"Next time," Tess said, "after we've caught a fish."

"Here, you hold the rod," Alison said. "Don't let go if it jerks suddenly."

"Okay," Tess said. She took the rod. "Do I let go if it's a shark?"

"Better hang on. My grandfather would be mad if you lost his rod," Alison said. She sat down, resting her back against a smooth slab of sun-warmed rock. "Come sit down. We might have a long wait."

They sat together and watched the float bob in the waves.

"So tell me about your friends at school," Tess asked.

Alison shrugged. "I hang around in this big group most of the time," she said. "There's a whole bunch of us—Renee, Melina, Keri, Angie, and Maria—who do things together. You know, eat lunch and go shopping."

"Are you very popular?" Tess asked.

Alison blushed. "I don't know," she said. "I have a lot of friends, but I'm just one of the group. Renee and Melina are sort of the leaders."

"Tell me about them," Tess said.

Alison thought for a moment. "They're both pretty and they always wear great clothes—unlike me, who has to wear what her mother chooses for her." Ali made a face, and Tess laughed.

"Are they nice?" Tess asked.

"They're nice, I guess," Ali answered.

"You guess?"

"They can be nice, if you're their friend." She didn't add, "if you do what they want."

Tess seemed to pick up what Alison hadn't said. "You don't sound like they're your best friends in the world," she said. "Why do you hang around with them?"

"I guess I like to belong," Alison said thoughtfully. "All my friends are in their clique. You know how it is, don't you?"

"Not really," Tess said. "I only hang around with people I like."

"I'm sort of scared of being left out, I guess," Ali said. She lay back for a moment, looking up at the sky. There were lots of kids at school who liked her, but nobody who was a real best friend —someone she could tell her deepest secrets and fears. She glanced across at Tess. "So how about you?" she asked. "Tell me about your friends at school."

"I hate school," Tess said quickly. "It's boring."

"All the time?"

"All the time," Tess said with a sigh. "I've been to so many schools. . . . Right now I go to this small private school. It's supposed to be great for expressing yourself and the sort of stuff Max thinks is important. You get to do what you want all the time."

"But that sounds great!" Alison said. "How could it be boring?"

Tess pushed her hair back again. Alison had noticed that she did this when she was angry or upset. She put both hands under it and lifted it, like a blanket, back off her shoulders. "They always want to do such babyish things," Tess said. "In English, we were reading this book about whaling ships in the Arctic. The other kids voted to build igloos out of sugar cubes instead of reading another book. We spent months and months playing with sugar cubes, when I wanted us to read *MacBeth*!"

Alison stole a sideways glance at Tess. Personally she would rather have built the sugar-cube igloo. That sounded much better than reading.

"Well, won't you be going to junior high in the fall?" she asked.

Tess sighed. "No, this school goes through eighth grade. Imagine, two more years of sugar-cube igloos!" Suddenly, the fishing rod jerked in her hands. She gave a squeal. "I've got one! Ali, I've got a fish! What do I do?" The line was bobbing up and down crazily.

"Reel it in very slowly," Alison said. "Gently, or it will pull off the hook and you'll lose it."

"I can't believe it, my first fish," Tess yelled.

It seemed to take forever to wind the line in. Finally, a silvery mackerel broke the surface and came flying up onto the rock beside the girls. "What do we do now?" Tess asked.

"Take the hook out carefully," Alison said, not adding that this was another part she usually got Grandpa to do.

The mackerel lay flopping and gasping on the rock. "But it's still alive," Tess said. "Why's it doing that?"

"It can't breathe out of the water," Alison said. "Do you want me to take it off the hook for you?"

"Yes," Tess said, jumping back as if to get away from the fish. "Put it back, Ali."

"What?"

"Throw it back in the water!"

"But Tess, it's your first fish," Alison said. "You could have it for lunch!"

"I don't want it for lunch," Tess said, sounding dangerously close to tears. "Poor thing. It's dying. Put it back!"

Alison knelt down and picked up the slippery, wriggling fish. She tried to remove the hook without hurting it, suddenly conscious of the creature's suffering. Finally she got it out, but not without tearing the fish's mouth.

"Oh, look. You've hurt it," Tess wailed.

"I couldn't help it. That's the only way to get the hook out," Alison said.

"Throw it back, please," Tess begged. Alison

held the silvery body in her hands, noticing how brilliant the silver and blue scales flashed in the sunlight. It was as if Tess had opened her eyes to a new way of looking at things. For the first time she saw the fish, not as something to be eaten at lunch, but as a creature with a right to live. She threw it out into the water. There was a splash, and it disappeared.

"Do you think its mouth will get better?" Tess asked.

"Definitely," Alison said.

"I wouldn't like to think of it swimming around with a torn mouth," Tess said.

"Better than ending up in bread crumbs," Alison commented, and Tess's face broke into a big grin.

"Thanks for saving it," she said.

"Just don't tell Grandpa," Alison muttered.

When Grandpa called to say he was ready to go home, they gathered up their lines and fell into step behind him.

"Any luck?" he asked.

Two heads shook.

"Me neither," he said. "Nothing biting today, I guess."

Ali and Tess exchanged a smile at the thought of their secret.

Chapter 6

"So what will we have for lunch now that there's no fish?" Tess asked as they made their way back to the house.

Alison realized that Tess was taking it for granted she could stay. "I'll ask my grandmother if you can eat with us," Ali said.

"Don't tell me," Tess said with a wicked grin. "It's Friday, so it must be croquet day, or maybe clam-digging day, or checkers, or . . ."

"It's not my fault I'm stuck with such a dumb family," Alison said, racing ahead.

"Hey, I didn't mean to upset you," Tess said, running to keep pace with her. "And I don't think your family is dumb. I think they're great—from a different planet maybe, but definitely great! I'd love to have a family like yours."

"Sometimes it's okay," Ali agreed. "But sometimes it drives me crazy! You should see when all the aunts and uncles and cousins are here. It's totally crazy. When they all come for my birthday party this Sunday . . ." Her face lit up.

"Hey, do you want to come to my birthday party? It's Sunday afternoon."

"It's your birthday this Sunday?" Tess asked. "Do you have a lot of friends coming?"

"*No* friends. Just family," Ali said. "It's always just family. Some of my relatives drive down from Philadelphia for the day." She hesitated. "It would be nice to have a friend of my own for once."

"Do you think your mom would mind?"

Ali hesitated. Tess had a point. Her mother might not want an outsider at a family party.

"I want you to come," Ali said. "That's what matters, isn't it?"

"Then tell her it's *your* party," Tess said.

"Okay," Ali said. "I will. Can you come?"

"I don't know. I'll have to check my busy schedule," Tess said. Then she burst out laughing. "You goob. Of course I'll come."

"Great," Ali said. "Now, let's go have lunch. I'm starving, how about you?"

Ali's mother looked concerned when Ali told her Tess was staying for lunch.

"But what about your parents, Tess?" she asked. "Won't they be expecting you to eat at home?"

"I doubt it," Tess said.

"I think you should call them anyway, just to

ask permission," Mrs. Hinkle said, picking up the phone.

Tess took the phone from her. "I don't think anyone will answer, though. My parents never answer phones when they're working."

She let the phone ring several times, then shrugged her shoulders as she put it down. Alison saw her mother looking strangely at Tess.

"Her family doesn't keep very regular hours like we do," Ali said before Tess could say any more. "Artists don't."

Mrs. Hinkle nodded as if this was probably true. "Well, you're very welcome to stay," she said.

After lunch, everyone went down to the beach. The day had become sticky and hot. Josh headed straight for the ocean and swam out with powerful strokes.

"Wow, your brother sure swims well," Tess commented.

"Want to take the rafts out?" Alison asked.

They carried the rubber rafts out past the waves and lay floating on the calm water. When their hands broke the surface, it was like breaking blue glass.

"Maybe your brother will teach me to swim better," Tess said, swiveling her raft around so that she could watch Josh. "He's a terrific athlete."

"I know," Ali agreed. "He's always winning medals for things at school, when he's not making honor roll or getting the lead in the play."

"I bet you're proud of him," Tess said.

Alison sighed and let her hand trail into the cool water. "Yeah, well it's not easy coming after him," she said. "I think they used up all the good genes on Josh. When I came along, there were only ordinary ones left."

"But you're good at things, too," Tess said.

"Name one," Alison demanded.

"I don't know all the things you can do yet," Tess said. "You can put worms on hooks."

"Oh, gee," Alison said dryly. "They don't give out many medals for that."

Tess giggled. "See, you're funny. You say funny things."

"I don't mean them to be funny, so it doesn't count," Alison said. "My back's starting to burn. Is yours?"

"I never burn," Tess said. "My genes are as bad as yours for not making honor roll, but they're great for not getting sunburnt. I've got some Italian and even a little bit Cherokee Indian, Maggie says, although I don't know if it's true or not."

"All I've got are things like Scottish and English and German," Alison said, swishing her hand through the water. "My genes aren't even any good for sunbathing! All I get is freckles and a peeling nose."

"But your hair gets blond streaks in it," Tess said. "That's worth having freckles."

"Nothing is worth freckles," Alison said. "I hate them. I've tried every way I know to get rid of them, but nothing works."

"Cover them up with makeup," Tess said. "That's what girls at my school do."

Alison looked up from her raft and laughed. "You've seen my mother! Do you think she'd let me wear makeup? You should have seen her when I put the teeniest bit of mascara on my eyelashes so that they'd look like eyelashes and not pale fuzz. She made me go right back to the bathroom and wash my face, and I missed my bus for school."

"What a bummer," Tess said. "Maggie lets me wear what I like. She wouldn't make a fuss if I bleached my hair or plucked my eyebrows or anything. She says that it's very important for a person to find herself through self-expression."

"You're lucky to have a mother like Maggie," Ali said.

"Oh, sure," Tess said. "It's really great." She lifted her hair off her shoulders with her familiar nervous gesture. "I think my back's starting to burn, too," she said quickly, and she began paddling toward the shore, leaving Alison to follow.

She had never met anyone who switched moods as quickly as Tess.

Robbie was knee-deep in sand, making one of his cities.

"Come and look at this, Ali," he called out. "It's the best one I've made all summer."

Alison admired the system of waterways, bridges, walls, and towers. Tess came over, too, and stood by Ali. "What happens to it when the tide comes in?" she asked.

"I'm going to build a wall," Robbie said. "If I make it big enough, the tide will go around and not get the city. You want to help?"

"Robbie, we're too old for sand castles," Alison said at the same time as Tess said, "Sure, why not?" Tess got down on her hands and knees. "Where do you want to start?"

She grabbed a spade and started digging furiously. "Don't just stand there. Dig!" she commanded as Alison continued to watch. "We need all the help we can get if we're going to beat the tide."

"You're crazy," Ali said, squatting down beside them. "You know the ocean's going to win."

"Maybe not this time," Tess said seriously. "Come on. I'll dig and you pat down."

They threw themselves into digging and patting. Sand flew everywhere. "Hey," Robbie shouted, "you're getting it all over me!" He started shoveling in their direction so that there was a miniature sandstorm.

The first waves broke at the wall, and a portion of it slid away.

"Quick, build it up again!" Tess yelled.

They all dug furiously but each successive wave took away more of the wall.

"I know," Tess yelled. "We'll sacrifice our bodies. Lie down next to me, Ali! We'll make a human wall and keep out the waves."

Tess lay on the sand in front of the wall. A wave broke over her, but most of it ran around the wall and the city stood. Robbie squealed happily. "Come on," Tess called. "My body's not enough."

Ali joined her. Waves ran into them, splashed over them. Robbie danced up and down excitedly. "Waves can't get my city!" he yelled, waving his spade. At last an enormous wave rushed in, bowling over Ali and Tess in a turmoil of foam and sand and water, and wiping out the city as it swept past. Ali and Tess picked themselves up, coughing and spluttering and laughing.

"Sorry, Rob," Tess said, looking at the smooth sand where the city had been. "I guess our bodies weren't enough."

"That's okay. My city lasted much longer than it usually does," Robbie said happily. "You want to go up to the house for some ice cream?"

"Sure," Tess said. "Race you to the gate!"

They set off, squealing over the dunes. Ali watched Tess's light, strong legs carry her across the sand. She could see that Tess was running slowly enough to let Robbie keep up with her, and she smiled. Tess had a way of turning an ordinary day at the beach into something special. *It's going to be a terrific summer!* Ali decided, breaking into a run to race after them.

Chapter 7

On Sunday afternoon, as Alison's family gathered for the party, Alison wasn't so sure she should have invited Tess after all. She recalled details of her past birthday parties and realized that they would seem weird even to a girl who trained rabbits. The more she thought about it, the more she wanted to call Tess and tell her not to come. So many little traditions that seemed normal to Alison's family would seem silly to someone as sophisticated as Tess.

Alison's mom had suspected the same thing when she heard that Ali had invited Tess.

"I think she might feel overwhelmed by a big, noisy family like ours. She doesn't really know us yet, and she might feel out of place," she had said.

"I don't care," Ali had said defiantly. "I want her to come. Anyway, I've already asked her."

Ali's mother had ruffled her hair. "All right, Little Alligator, keep your hair on," she had said.

"And please stop calling me that in front of

54

my friends," Ali had said, dodging away from her mother. "It's so embarrassing."

She had fought a small battle with her mother and won. But as the first guests arrived, laughing noisily in the front hall, she began to suspect that her mother might have been right.

Tess, wearing a black leather miniskirt and a lacy white peasant blouse, had arrived just before all the relatives. Ali thought she looked very nice and grown up, but she saw her mother raise an eyebrow at her father.

"You look so nice," Ali said loudly to Tess. "I wish I could wear clothes that didn't make me look like an eight-year-old."

"You look nice, too," Tess said.

"If you happen to enjoy looking like Shirley Temple," Ali muttered, and they exchanged a grin. Ali was conscious that her own dress was very young-looking. It was pink lace with a dropped waist and two little pink roses at the hip. Her mother had swept her hair back from her face with a pink silk headband and then curled it so it cascaded down her back in soft waves.

"Don't you look lovely," Grandma exclaimed as Alison came out to meet her guests.

"Who is this beautiful young woman?" Uncle Dave asked. "A guest of yours, Helen?" He bowed to Alison. "Pardon me, miss, but have you seen Alison Hinkle anywhere? I'd like to give her a birthday hug."

"Oh, Uncle Dave," Alison said with an embarrassed giggle.

Uncle Dave gave an astonished look around the room. "Don't tell me this is Alison! I can't believe it. She's all grown up."

"She's not too old for her bumps, is she?" Todd, her ten-year-old cousin, asked hopefully.

"Bumps? You're never too old for bumps in this family," Alison's father said.

"Grandpa doesn't get them," Todd's little brother Mark commented.

Grandpa laughed. "That's because nobody can toss me in the air seventy-five times!"

Alison's dad stepped into the middle of the room. "Clear a space, everyone. Alison's getting her bumps. Come on, Josh, Dave, Sue—we'll need all the help we can get this year. She's getting heavy."

"I am not!" Alison said indignantly. Hands grabbed her arms and legs, sweeping her off her feet. "One . . . two . . . three," they shouted as they tossed her into the air and caught her again. When they got to twelve they dropped her, not very gently, on the floor. Everyone cheered. Alison got up and straightened her dress just as Grandma appeared in the doorway with a beautiful pink cake in her hands.

"Come on, Tess," Ali said, because Tess was hanging back. "You can sit beside me."

She took Tess's hand and led her to the dining room, where a beautiful table had been set. It was decorated with fresh flowers and candles and piled high in the middle with presents. Ali sat in the big chair usually reserved for Grandpa. Grandpa put a silver paper crown on Alison's head. "I crown you queen for the day," he said solemnly. Ali's father lit the candles and they all sang "Happy Birthday" in the same boisterous and out-of-tune way they always did.

Alison leaned over the cake and blew out the candles. As she did she caught Tess's eye. Tess looked as if she might burst out laughing at any moment. Ali realized how ridiculous the whole ritual was, and she, too, had to hold in her laughter.

"I've never seen so many presents for one person," Grandpa said. "What a spoiled child. Now, when I was growing up—"

"We know, Grandpa," Josh interrupted. "All you got for your birthday was an apple."

"No, it was a crust of dry bread," Todd yelled.

Alison looked across at Tess and found herself wishing that Tess hadn't come to the party after all. During earlier summers, Ali had always loved being the center of attention, queen for a day, as Grandpa put it. She had always looked forward to opening all her presents, making sure she didn't rip the paper on the last one so she wouldn't get tickled. She had even loved the big game of hide-and-seek and the family sing-along that were part of the birthday tradition. But now all those things seemed embarrassing. Tess made Ali see things differently, and now she saw that she was too old for family birthday parties. It was as if Tess had pricked a special balloon that could never be blown up again.

When the party was finally over, Ali walked Tess to the door.

"See, what did I tell you," she said. "Talk about an overpowering family."

"It was interesting," Tess said. "I felt like an anthropologist watching a family of chimpanzees."

"Gee, thanks a lot."

Tess laughed. "I didn't mean you were monkeys. I meant that it was so totally different from my own life. From most other lives, too, I guess. I mean, who else has uncles that crawl around on the floor and grandparents who sing duets?" She launched into an imitation of Ali's grandpa singing.

"I think they sound pretty good," Ali said shortly. "They always sing that song at parties."

"Sorry, I didn't mean to upset you," Tess said.

"It was really interesting . . . and you got some neat stuff."

"Yeah, the loot wasn't bad this year," Alison said. "I never thought my grandparents would give me a new bike. I thought I'd be stuck with the bike with the flowery basket forever."

Tess paused and then swallowed. "Look, Ali, I'm sorry I didn't get you a present," she said. "Maggie promised to take me into town yesterday, then she sort of took off without me for the day. I guess she forgot."

"It's okay," Ali said. "Having you here was good enough for me."

"I'll get you a present as soon as someone will drive me into town," Tess said.

"It's okay. You don't have to," Ali insisted.

"But I want to," Tess said. Her face lit up in a wicked grin. "And do you know why? Because it will be your very last present, Little Alligator, and if you rip the paper, you know what will happen to you, don't you? Tickle, tickle, tickle."

"Don't," Ali said, dodging away. "It's bad enough that they do it!"

"Sorry," Tess said, still smiling. "Hey, want to put your new bike to good use and show me around Rose Bay tomorrow?"

"Sure," Alison said. "I'll come over in the morning." She was thinking that she hadn't seen the inside of Tess's house since the redecorating was finished. She was curious to see what Tess's life was like—with famous, creative parents and a schedule you could make up yourself.

She tried to imagine what it would be like, dressing in her black leather miniskirt and going out, anywhere she wanted, without telling *anybody. Freedom!*, she thought. *What wouldn't I give to make my own decisions.*

On Monday morning, Alison rode her new bike to Tess's house right after breakfast. She was really looking forward to escaping from her family for the day.

It was only as she rode into Tess's front yard and heard a piano being played that she remembered Tess's life included a scary father. What if she had to face Tess's dad? She already knew that he got mad easily. She remembered how he had yelled at the piano movers and at Tess's mom. What if Tess was still asleep and her dad got angry at being interrupted?

But, luckily, as she wheeled her bike slowly to the front door she heard her name and turned to see Tess, beside the house, busy with a pile of wood.

"I'm making Rajah a super-deluxe condominium," she called to Ali.

Ali propped up her bike and ran up the steps

onto the porch. "I thought I'd have to wake you up."

Tess made a face. "With that noise?" she asked. "He started at seven."

Ali glanced toward the house. "Is his music always like that?"

Tess busied herself with the hammer. "Only at the moment," she said. "He didn't want to come here. It was Maggie's idea, so he's making her pay for it."

"Oh," Alison said. She couldn't imagine her own father or mother acting so childishly.

Maggie appeared on the porch behind them. She was wearing an oversize tie-dyed shirt that came almost down to her knees and blue jeans. She had a streak of blue paint across her nose. Her face was pale and her eyes seemed puffy and red, the way Alison's looked when she had been crying.

"I've made some tea," she said to Tess and Ali. "Do you want some?"

"Okay," Tess said. "I haven't had breakfast yet." She got to her feet. "Come on, Ali. Let's see what there is to eat."

"Not much," Maggie said. "I was out painting all day yesterday. We really need to go to the store."

Ali followed Tess into the house. It was hardly

more furnished than the last time she had seen it. Some bright handwoven rugs now lay on the hardwood floors, and a huge wool hanging that looked like a partially unwound sheep was now over the mantelpiece. On the walls were several big paintings of straggly lines and blobs in oranges and reds. Alison guessed they were Maggie's. Max was still playing the piano and didn't look up as they came in.

Maggie went over to him. "You've been playing since dawn," she said. "You could at least stop long enough to say hello to your daughter and her friend."

Max stopped and looked up as if he wasn't quite sure where he was. He looked around and seemed to fasten his gaze on Alison for the first time. "Oh, hi there," he said as if he'd never seen her before.

"After all," Maggie went on sweetly, "you were the one who claimed that you had to have people around you to work, didn't you?"

"That's me, Mr. Sociability." He turned to Tess. "You want to introduce us?"

"Alison, this is my dad, Max Neville," Tess said with a funny bow.

Max gave Alison a sort of half-smile. "Hi, Alison, how are you?" he asked. "So what are you girls planning to do today?"

"Have breakfast first," Tess said. "I'm starving."

Max glanced across at his wife. "I don't think you'll find much food in the house," he said. "Nobody's been to the store."

"I thought you said you'd go yesterday," she said.

"I forgot. I had other things on my mind," he said.

"I could have gone if you'd asked me," Maggie said. She was still speaking in a sweet, even voice, but underneath, Alison thought it sounded angry. She bit her lip as she glanced across at Tess. Tess didn't look at all upset.

"It's okay," Tess said. "I'll find something." She started to walk into the kitchen. Alison gratefully turned to follow her, but Max called after them.

"Why don't you girls go into town and get something to eat? It's about time you had a good day out." He reached into his pocket. "Here's ten bucks. Would that do it?"

"Gee, thanks," Tess said, taking the money.

"Oh, Max," Maggie cut in. "There will only be greasy hamburger places and ice cream at the beach! You know I don't like her eating that stuff."

"She's only a kid once, Maggie," Max said, "and she hasn't had much fun for a while, has she?" He winked at Tess. "Go enjoy yourself, okay?"

"Sure. Thanks, Max," Tess said.

"See if you can find some frozen yogurt," Maggie called after them. Before Tess had a chance to close the door, they heard Maggie say to Max in that same sweet but icy voice, "You only did that to spite me. You know I don't like her eating fast food!"

Tess banged the door shut. "Ugh, parents," she said. "They are so childish."

Alison was grateful to get away. She had never been in a household where adults fought in front of strangers. She wondered how much Tess minded their fighting. She didn't look upset, but it was hard to tell what she was thinking. Freedom or no freedom, Ali realized that Tess's life was not as great as she had first thought.

"I'm in the mood for a big, juicy hamburger," Tess said. "How about you?" Tess gave Ali a big smile, but Ali noticed that her eyes were extra bright, as if she were only one step away from tears. Ali wanted to let Tess know that she understood what she was going through, but she couldn't think of the right thing to say. "A hamburger now?" she said. "I don't think . . ." She was about to add that no place in Rose Bay would be likely to serve hamburgers before ten o'clock in the morning. But when she looked at Tess's face again, she could tell that the hamburger was important to her. "A big, juicy hamburger. Good idea!" she said. "Go get your bike."

Chapter 8

As Ali had suspected, the food stand at the beach was not selling hamburgers when they arrived at Rose Bay. The snack-bar owner, a fat man wearing a greasy white apron over a big belly, scowled at Tess and Ali.

"Can't you read?" he grumbled. "It says open from eleven to four."

Ali shrank back, but Tess spoke up. "You don't seem too busy," she said. "Couldn't you just cook us a couple of hamburgers as a special favor?"

The man looked as if he might explode. "I don't do special favors for nobody. Now, beat it."

Tess grabbed Ali's arm. "What a mean man," she said, turning to scowl back at him. "I bet his hamburgers are too greasy anyway! Where else can we try?"

"I think there's a fast-food place at the miniature golf course," Ali said. "But it probably doesn't open until lunchtime either."

"Then I guess we'll have to do something until

lunchtime," Tess said. "You can give me my guided tour of Rose Bay now."

"That won't take long," Ali said. "You're looking at the whole thing. That's the beach and that's the jetty, and the pool's behind that fence, and there's the store where they sell the saltwater taffy. You want to get some taffy to keep you going until we find a hamburger?"

"Sure," Tess said. "We can eat it while we check out the famous sites of Rose Bay, like the lifeguards."

They stood outside the store, watching the taffy machine stretch and turn the bright pink taffy over and over. Then they bought a bag and walked down onto the jetty, not speaking as they chewed.

"This is great," Tess managed to say at last. "I think I pulled out all my fillings, but it was worth it." She looked across at Ali and grinned. "Maggie would have a fit if she saw me eating this!"

"My mom's not too crazy about it either," Ali said.

Tess made a face. "Parents. Who needs 'em?" she said, but Ali noticed that she no longer looked depressed. She swallowed the last of her candy and leaned over the side of the jetty. A fishing boat had just come in, and men were unloading two enormous fish. The giant bodies glinted with rainbow sparkles in the bright morning sun.

"Look, Ali, they're huge," Tess said. "Poor things. I wish we could have rescued them like we did our little mackerel."

"Have another piece of taffy," Ali said, offering Tess the bag.

They went down onto the beach, kicking off their sneakers and sinking into the fine golden sand. The beach was deserted except for a few families with little kids and a couple of college-aged kids playing volleyball. The girls walked down to the water's edge and stood, knee-deep, as the waves rushed past them. Wading in the ocean with her new friend, Ali felt a wonderful sense of freedom.

After a while, Tess announced, "I'm starving. How far is it to the miniature golf?"

"About a mile down the beach path," Ali said, She curled her toes into the sand.

"Let's go then," Tess said. "Maybe they're open. Aren't you starving, too?"

"I'm not really allowed to go that far," Ali mumbled.

"You're not alone. You've got me with you," Tess said.

"I know," Ali said, "But I should really call home and get permission."

"What if they say no? Then I'll die of starvation. You wouldn't want that, would you? And we could play miniature golf if the hamburgers aren't ready."

"I really want to go," Ali said hesitantly.

"Then just go," Tess said. "You're twelve years old. You can make up your own mind."

Ali thought of juicy hamburgers and miniature golf and a long bike ride with Tess. "You're right," Ali said. "I am old enough to make up my own mind."

"What are we waiting for?" Tess yelled excitedly. "Hamburgers, here we come!"

They hurried back to their bikes. The pedals on Ali's new bike turned effortlessly. She was enjoying the wonderful feeling of speed. The breeze in her face smelled of ocean. She felt free and grown up, and it was wonderful.

Their faces were both bright pink when they reached the flashing sign that said "Magicland Miniature Golf." The entrance was shaped like a castle. The fast-food stand next door had a sign that said "Open for Lunch" on it.

"I guess it's got to be golf first," Tess said with a shrug.

Tess paid for them, and they started working their way around the golf course.

"I sure hope I get my hamburger," Tess said as she whacked her ball through an old castle and heard it clang down the other side. "If I go home again, I bet there still won't be any food in the house. It will be a battle of wills. Neither of them will want to go out and get food first."

Alison looked at the back of Tess's head as she bent to hit the ball again. Her long dark hair fell across her face, and she looked very small. Ali had no idea what Tess might be going through, but she thought that maybe talking about it would make her feel better.

"Have your parents been fighting a lot?" she asked.

Tess reached for her ball and shook her hair back. "I don't want to talk about it," she said.

Ali followed. "Sometimes it helps."

Tess shook her head. For the next three holes she was very quiet. Then they came to a hole where the object was to hit the ball through the open mouth of a crouching grizzly bear. Tess let out a loud laugh.

"Hey, Ali, doesn't that remind you of your uncle Dave when he was playing hide-and-seek yesterday? He looked so dumb crouching behind that sofa! I thought I'd die. Boy, you have the weirdest family. . . . All those stupid games . . . and the bumps . . ." She went on laughing.

"I told you they were weird," Ali said uncomfortably. "All those things at the party are things they used to do when my dad was young. I can't change them now."

Tess picked up her ball and skipped ahead. "You'll never catch me now," she said. "Just the dragon and the volcano and I'm done."

Alison followed slowly, feeling hurt and confused. Tess knew she already felt embarrassed by her party. Why did she have to tease her about it? Being with Tess was like being on a roller coaster! One minute she was having more fun, feeling more free, than she ever had in her whole life, and the next minute Tess would say something mean and make her feel terrible. This wasn't the way friends were supposed to be, was it?

"I think I finally smell hamburgers cooking, don't you?" Tess called as Ali finished the last hole.

She gave Ali an excited smile, as if she had completely forgotten how mean she had been. "I hope the hamburgers are juicy and full of cholesterol."

The mention of cholesterol reminded Ali suddenly of home. She glanced at her watch. It was past eleven-thirty, and she was two miles from home.

"Tess! I can't stay for a hamburger," she said. "I have to be home for lunch."

"Ali, you can't!" Tess wailed. "I've been looking forward to this hamburger all morning. It won't be any fun unless you eat one with me."

"But they're expecting me," Ali said.

A delicious smell of onions and cooking meat came from the hamburger stand.

"So call and tell them you're eating lunch here," Tess said as if this was the easiest thing in the world.

"I don't know . . . ," Ali said.

"They won't mind," Tess insisted. "It will be all the more food for everyone else. Josh will eat yours. I'll call for you if you're scared."

That settled it for Ali. "I'll call," she said.

Josh answered the phone. "Tell Mom I'm eating lunch with Tess," she said and hung up before he could say anything. The hamburgers tasted twice as juicy as any hamburger she had ever eaten.

Chapter 9

By midafternoon the sky, which had been completely blue all morning, suddenly began to cloud over. Great gray banks hung over the ocean, turning into gray towers and mountains as they rushed in toward the land. Alison and Tess, stomachs full from hamburgers and jaws aching from the last of the saltwater taffy, had been busy watching and giggling over the boys on the high dive at the pool. They didn't notice the storm until there was a rumble of thunder out at sea.

"Oh, no. Was that thunder?" Ali asked. "Hey, look at the sky."

They started running toward their bikes. "We're going to have to ride home in a hurry or we'll get soaked," Tess shouted.

"Maybe we should wait until it passes over," Ali called back. "There's no shelter between Rose Bay and home."

"Nah, we can beat it," Tess said. "We'll just ride fast. Besides, a little rain won't hurt us."

"You don't know what the lightning can be

like out here. I really think we should wait and see," Ali said.

"You're not scared of lightning, are you?" Tess asked.

"Of course not."

"Then let's try and beat it," Tess said. She put on a sweet smile. "Come on, Little Alligator."

"Shut up," Ali said, laughing at Tess's imitation of her mother.

"Race ya," Tess yelled.

"Okay," Ali yelled back. "You won't beat me! I've got a new bike!"

She ran and jumped on her bike, pedaling as fast as she could. She could hear the swish of Tess's tires beside her. She switched gears as the track became sandy. They had barely left Rose Bay when the rain started. Not just a gentle pattering but a downpour, as if someone had spilled a bucket over their heads.

Ali could see Tess's excited face beside her, and suddenly she caught Tess's excitement. The wind was behind her now, sweeping her along, pushing as if it were a giant hand. Faster and faster she pedaled, almost as if she were flying. Her wheels were singing on the track, and spray was flying up in all directions. Tess moved ahead of her, and Tess's spray came up in Ali's face, making her gasp. She put on extra effort and sprayed Tess back. Tess squealed and yelled something, but it was swallowed up in the storm.

Thunder growled nearer, and Alison saw lightning flicker out at sea.

When thunder crashed almost overhead, she began to feel scared. Tess was still beside her, head down, red-faced and pedaling hard. She didn't look scared at all.

Suddenly, the shape of Alison's house loomed out of the rain in front of them.

"You know what?" Tess yelled as they screeched to a halt on the gravel of Alison's driveway.

"What?"

"We didn't beat it," she said. They looked at each other and burst into laughter.

As Ali wheeled her bike into the shed, the laughter faded. She realized that her mother would not find this at all funny. Now that she was tired and cold, she really didn't want a long lecture from her mother.

"What's the matter?" Tess asked.

"My mom's going to kill me, that's all," Ali said.

"You want to go to my house first and dry off?" Tess asked.

A loud crash of thunder made Ali jump. "No," she said. "I'll have to face her sometime."

"Tell her she's lucky you're not a fried alligator," Tess said. She started giggling again.

Alison's mother and grandmother were sitting together at the kitchen table when the girls came in. The women were busy stoning plums and throwing them into a huge cooking pot.

"Mercy me," Grandmother said. "You look like two drowned rats."

"Where have you been?" her mother asked. "We were getting worried about you."

"Just down at the beach," Ali said. "I showed Tess Rose Bay, and her dad treated us to lunch."

Her mother was shaking her head. "And you rode home in this storm? Alison, I thought you were more sensible than that!"

"Why didn't you wait in the store until it passed over, or call your grandpa to come and get you?" Grandma asked. "You're lucky you weren't both struck by lightning!"

Ali looked across at Tess. She half expected Tess to say, "It was my idea to ride home in the rain. Ali wanted to wait." But she didn't.

"I'm surprised at you, Alison," her mother said. "You're normally so responsible."

"It's no big deal, Mom," Ali said, angry at all of them.

"No big deal?" Mrs. Hinkle demanded. "Alison, there's a storm out there. It's thundering."

"It wasn't raining when we started from Rose

Bay, okay?" Alison snapped. "We were halfway here, and it would have been dumb to turn back. We didn't think a little rain would hurt us."

"There's no need to be rude." Mrs. Hinkle was already pushing them toward the stairs. "I just hope you don't catch cold now. Look at you both shivering. Take Tess upstairs and let her take a warm shower before she catches pneumonia. Come on, let me find you both towels."

"I can find my own towels. You don't have to treat me like a baby all the time," Alison said abruptly. "I'm old enough to look after myself, you know."

"Obviously not, if you decide to ride home in a lightning storm," Ali's mother called after her.

"We made it, didn't we?" Ali said, turning back. "Nothing terrible happened to us!" She nudged Tess. "Come on, Tess," she said. "Let's go take a shower."

Tess was giggling. She looked across at Ali, her eyes sparkling through wet lashes. "We already took a shower," she said. Ali headed quickly in the direction of the stairs. She pressed her lips together so that she didn't start laughing, too. Her mother wouldn't think it was at all funny. She would probably say that Tess was a bad influence. *But I think she's a very good influence on me,* Ali thought. *I'm finally learning to take some risks and have a good time!*

When they got to the top of the stairs, she looked across at Tess and grinned back.

"Find Tess some of your clothes to wear," her mother called after them. "And bring hers down to put in the dryer."

"See what I mean? They make such a fuss about everything," Ali whispered to Tess.

"But it's nice that they care about you," Tess said. "They don't want you to catch pneumonia!"

"They didn't want *you* to catch pneumonia, remember? I could die from frostbite as long as I come home on time," Ali said, giving Tess a push that started her laughing again.

"Did you see their faces when we came in! You'd have thought we were aliens."

"It's all right for you," Ali said, still fighting her giggles. "My mom will haunt me with this for the rest of my life. She'll make me wear a raincoat every time I go out now. Every time I sneeze, she'll remind me that I wouldn't be sneezing if I hadn't ridden home in the rain."

"If it bugs you, tell her to quit babying you," Tess said seriously.

Ali glanced back down the stairs to see if her mother was still within hearing range. Luckily, she wasn't.

"It's not that easy," she said. "You saw how I tried to explain."

78

You have to be more firm," Tess said. "Just stand up to her and say, 'I'm twelve years old and I'm not a baby anymore, so stop trying to rule my life!'"

"It wouldn't work," Ali said with a sigh.

"What would she do, lock you in your room? Ground you for life?"

"Worse than that," Ali said. "She'd laugh and ruffle my hair. Then she'd just keep treating me exactly the same way. She doesn't take me seriously."

"You're going to have to put your foot down sometime," Tess said. "Or she'll be following you to college and choosing your roommate."

"I know," Ali said. "I wish I had a mother like Maggie who let me do exactly what I wanted. You want to trade?"

"It's not as great as you think," Tess said. "At least you know your mother will be around when you need her."

"What do you mean?" Ali asked. "Is Maggie going somewhere?"

Tess frowned. "I just meant that she's always taking off to art shows." She paused. "Would you hurry up and get me that towel? I'm freezing."

Ali opened the linen closet and took out two large towels. "The shower's down the hall," she said. "I'll find you a robe."

She took out her robe for Tess, then began to

79

peel off her own soaked clothing. Her hands were cold and numb, which made it difficult to unfasten the buttons on her shorts. She was down to her underwear when Tess came in, wrapped in her towel.

"I hurried as fast as I could because I knew you'd be freezing, and we don't want you to catch cold, do we, Little Alligator!" Tess giggled.

Alison gave her a look as she wrapped herself in a towel.

"Oh, good," Tess interrupted. "You don't wear a bra either. I thought I was the only flat person in the world."

"I'll need one soon," Ali said.

"I'll need one soon, too," Tess said, "but neither of us needs one right now. Some of the girls in my class at school stuff their bras with tissues. I'd never do that, would you?"

"No way," Ali said, shocked. She made a rapid list of the girls in her class and wondered which of those shapes were due to tissues. Funny how little she really knew about her school friends.

"Me neither," Tess said. "I don't think I want to grow up."

"Oh, I do," Ali said. "I can't wait to be able to do things without asking permission."

Tess wrapped the towel around her head and began to rub her hair dry. "I hope you have some designer clothes for me to wear, Dahling, because

I'm very picky." She spoke in a movie-star voice and did a slinky walk over to the closet.

Then she seemed to notice the room for the first time. "What a neat room!" she exclaimed. "It's so spooky. Is it haunted?"

"I don't think so," Ali said. "My grandpa had this house built. Nobody's ever died in it. . . ."

"You never know," Tess said. "Maybe a ship was wrecked right here and the ghosts of the sailors were lingering until someone built a house, or maybe it's on the site of an old Indian burial ground. Are you sure you've never woken and found an Indian standing over your bed?"

"Yes," Alison said, half laughing, half scared. She glanced around her room. She had always thought of it as a friendly room until now. In the half-darkness of the storm, with the rattling windowpanes and moaning wind, it did seem spooky.

"It sure feels haunted to me," Tess said. "I bet that funny old door in the wall leads somewhere. There's probably stuff hidden behind it."

"There is," Ali said, laughing now. "Old beach chairs and broken tennis racquets."

"Your problem is that you've got no imagination," Tess said, climbing up on Ali's bed to kneel and look out the window. Her face lit up. "Hey, I've got a great idea. How about if I spend the night tonight, since I'm already showered?" she asked.

"I don't know," Alison said. "I'll have to ask my mother."

"Don't you want me to?"

"Of course I do," Alison said. "It's just that my mother's funny about sleepovers. She claims I'm always grouchy in the morning because I don't get enough sleep."

"And are you?"

"Only after slumber parties when everyone stays up all night," Alison said. "I threw up once after a party, because we ate nonstop and stayed up all night watching movies. My mom always reminds me of that."

"But we wouldn't stay up all night, would we?" Tess asked, grinning wickedly.

"Nah!" Ali said, her own face lighting up, too. "Only till two o'clock, right?"

"Right," Ali said, "Two-thirty maximum. I'll skip my shower. I'm warm now, anyway. Let's go down and ask her."

A sudden gust of wind spattered rain on the window. "The weather's getting worse," Tess said. "That's a great excuse."

The girls scrambled down the stairs as quickly as they could, and Alison took the last three steps at a jump, just the way Tess did.

Chapter 10

Alison's mother and grandmother were still in the kitchen when the girls came downstairs. The sweet, sticky smell of stewing plums now came from the pot on the stove that Grandma was stirring. Alison's mother was lining up jars.

"Mom, can Tess sleep over?" Alison blurted out.

Her mother looked from Alison to Tess. "I don't know if that's a good idea, dear," she said. "You're always so grouchy in the morning. And remember that time you got sick?"

Ali heard Tess stifle a giggle. "That was when I stayed up all night at a party and ate too much, Mom," she said.

Ali could see Tess was about to laugh out loud and blow the whole thing. She dug Tess in the ribs. Luckily, Grandma intervened. "It looks like this storm is in for the night, Helen. Maybe it would be wise if she stayed here. She'd get soaked again on her way home, and we do have plenty of pot roast."

"Well . . ." Ali's mother looked thoughtful. "If you both promise to go to bed at a sensible time," she said, "I'll call Tess's mother and ask her. Do you think it will be all right with her, Tess? After all, she hardly knows us."

Tess grinned. "It will be fine," she said.

Alison was so excited to have Tess spend the night that she forgot all about the ghost until they had brushed their teeth and were getting ready for bed.

"We can do all sorts of neat stuff," Tess exclaimed. "We can sneak food upstairs for a midnight feast, or go down and watch TV, or wait up here to see the ghost."

"I told you, there's no ghost," Alison said. The wind outside was now moaning horribly, and there was a slapping sound as it lifted a tile from the roof. She found herself glancing over nervously to the dark corner beyond her bedside lamp.

"Let's turn the light out and wait for the ghost now," Tess whispered. "Then, when they've all gone to bed, we can sneak downstairs again and get a midnight snack."

She leaned over and switched the light out. The room was darker than Ali ever remembered it. "Oh, spirit of the other world, are you there?" Tess called in a low voice.

Ali sat in bed, hugging her knees, her eyes on

the pinpoint of light coming from the keyhole. She held her breath for a moment, waiting for the ghost to appear.

"See, I told you," she said, letting out a sigh of relief. "There's no ghost."

"Maybe he's shy," Tess said. "Or maybe I didn't say the right words yet. Maybe he's here but he can't materialize. Oh, spirit," she began again, "if you can't show yourself right now, give us a sign. Let us know of your presence. . . ."

As if in answer, there was a loud clatter right outside the window. Ali grabbed at Tess, even though she realized the noise was just a tile that had come loose in the storm and crashed to the ground.

"See, I was right," Tess said, but her voice sounded shaky now. "What did I tell you? I have a feeling for this sort of thing."

"It was only a tile," Alison said at last. "A tile fell from the roof."

"Or maybe the tile was the sign," Tess said, but Alison noticed that she didn't try to summon up the ghost again. Instead she said, "You want to sneak down and get our snack now?" "We could take down your quilt and pillows and watch TV."

"I guess," Alison said.

"Don't you want to?" Tess sounded surprised.

"Sure, but . . . ," Ali began.

"But what?"

"What if they catch us?"

"Come on, Ali," Tess said, dragging her off the bed. "It's no fun sleeping over if we don't do something exciting. Tell you what—if they catch us we'll say we were sleepwalking and just happened to walk to the pantry and sit down in front of the TV."

She looked at Alison, her eyes shining. "Okay," Ali said. She could feel the tight knot of excitement in her stomach. She had never watched TV after midnight before, and it did sound like fun.

They crept down the stairs, holding their breath each time a stair creaked. As they drew level with Ali's grandparents' bedroom on the first floor, a loud snore made them jump. They clamped their hands over their mouths to keep from exploding with laughter. They made it safely to the kitchen and piled a plate with chocolate-chip cookies from the baking jar and a piece of apple pie left from dinner.

"Just a light snack," Tess said, giggling.

"I hope I don't really throw up after all this," Ali said.

"Do you think your grandmother will miss this stuff?" Tess asked.

"I'll tell her you got hungry," Ali joked as they carried the food to the living room.

"I hope there's something good on," Tess whispered, switching on the TV set. "I hardly ever get to watch TV."

"Turn the sound way down or they'll hear us," Alison whispered back. Then she remembered that she hadn't seen a TV at Tess's house. "Don't you have one at home?"

"No!" Tess whispered back. "Max and Maggie say it stifles creativity. I guess they're right, but once in a while I'd love to watch cartoons in the afternoons like other kids."

Ali flicked through the channels until they came to the Late, Late Show.

"Hold it there," Tess instructed. "This looks good."

"And now back to our movie, *The Curse of the Mummy's Tomb*," the announcer said.

"I love horror movies, don't you?" Tess said, snuggling under the quilt. "This one is really good, too. I think I saw it once."

"I thought you didn't have a TV."

"Max and I go to horror movies all the time in New York," Tess said. "Maggie never comes with us. She says they're disgusting, but Max and I love them!"

Alison lay down on her tummy beside Tess. "This'll be great," she said. "I never get to see horror movies."

"Your mom won't let you, right?" Tess said at

the exact moment that Ali said, "My mom won't let me."

They both burst out laughing, and buried themselves under the quilt until they could stop.

"I hope it's not too scary," Ali said. "I get nightmares really easily."

"You do?" Tess said, wrinkling her nose. "I'm *never* scared."

"Never?"

"Well, not of dumb things like movies. It's only a bunch of actors wearing costumes," Tess said.

The eerie music got louder. A man and a woman were walking down a dark passageway. Suddenly a bat fluttered into their faces. Alison jumped and grabbed Tess.

"It was only a bat," Tess said. "Look, you made me drop pie crumbs on the carpet. It's not real, you know."

"I know," Alison said. Tess was obviously used to this sort of stuff, but Ali thought she might have tried to understand that some people did get scared, even though it *was* only a movie.

The two people on the screen continued down the passage. Then, around a corner, came this horrible thing, silently following the woman, trailing bandages, its mouth gaping open, closer and closer. Alison wanted to shut her eyes, but she couldn't. She was too scared to move. The music was throbbing now. The thing reached out its arm to grab the woman, and the arm just kept on growing and growing. Alison's heart was hammering so loudly, she was sure it would wake her family upstairs. She wanted to see if Tess was scared, but she didn't dare look away from the screen.

"It's only a story, it's not real. That's just a man wearing a mummy suit," she kept chanting to herself. She chanted it as the man opened the coffin and a horrible mummy pulled him inside.

Surely even Tess must be scared now, she thought. She glanced over, but Tess was nowhere to be seen! Alison's first thought was that the mummy had taken her away, just like in the movie. Then she spotted a lump way under the quilt. She pulled back the quilt and found Tess curled up in a little ball, pretending to be asleep.

"Oh, is it over?" Tess asked, stretching and yawning. "I got so bored that I must have fallen asleep."

"You weren't asleep," Alison accused. "I saw your eyelids flicker."

"I was just sort of dozing. I got sleepy."

"You got scared and you hid!"

"I did not!" Tess said. "Who would be scared of a stupid movie like that?" She looked at Alison, wide-eyed. "Don't tell me you were really scared!" Then she started to giggle.

"Shut up," Ali said, but Tess only went on giggling. Ali left her giggling and went up to bed.

"Hey, Ali, don't be mad. I didn't mean . . . ," Tess called after her, but Ali didn't stop. *Some friend,* she thought.

Chapter 11

Alison was too scared to sleep for the rest of the night. Every time she dozed off, she would shake herself awake in case a ghost or a mummy was coming in through the window. By morning she was tired and grouchy, just as her mother claimed she would be. Tess, on the other hand, was bright and bouncy. She seemed to have forgotten that Alison had gone to bed mad.

"So what are we going to do today?" she asked. "Go down and swim at the public pool? Talk to the cute lifeguards on the beach?"

"The weather's not good enough," Ali said. "It looks yucky out there. Besides, I don't feel too great."

Tess wagged a finger. "You see, my Little Alligator," she said, doing her famous mother imitation, "I told you what would happen if you let a friend sleep over. Now you're grounded for the next ten years."

She did the imitation so well that Alison had to smile, even though she was still feeling mad.

"It's not funny," she managed to say. "It will probably happen."

After breakfast, Tess went home to change and Ali stood in the shower, fighting with a turmoil of angry feelings. Was Tess her friend or wasn't she? They had so much fun together, and yet Tess didn't always act like a friend. Ali remembered the way Tess had teased her about her birthday party, her nickname, and her mother. She had let Ali take the blame for riding home in the storm, and then she had made fun of Ali's terror during the scary movie.

I bet she was scared, too, Ali thought, *only she couldn't admit it! I don't know if I want someone like that for a friend.*

Of course, when she thought about not seeing Tess anymore, Ali knew that wasn't what she wanted. Tess made her see life differently. She had shown her that life could be fun and exciting. Ali sighed. She wanted Tess to be the best friend she ever had. She wanted her to be perfect —not mean, not unpredictable, just perfect. *She's got to learn that she can't push me around anymore,* Ali thought.

Ali had just finished her shower when Tess called.

"Ali, can you come over?" she asked. "I want to work on Rajah's rabbit condo. The cage leaked last night, and I don't want him catching cold."

"I don't know. I've got things to do this morning," Ali said.

"What kind of things?"

"All sorts of things—family things," Ali said.

"But, Ali . . ." Tess's voice was pleading. "I'm all alone over here. Max has gone into town to get groceries, and Maggie's off painting somewhere. Rajah really needs his new cage. Are they very important things?"

"Sort of," Ali said, feeling herself weakening.

"It's no fun without you here," Tess said. "I'll make you my famous lunch special—peanut butter on rice crackers!"

"Maybe I'll be over later."

"Please make it sooner," Tess said.

"Okay," Ali finally agreed. "I guess I'll come over."

"Thanks, Al, you're the best friend I ever had," Tess said, making Ali feel warm inside.

She rode over to Tess's house, pushing the angry feelings to the back of her head.

"I couldn't make it go right," Tess said in a small voice when Ali arrived. "I was sure you'd know how to do it. After all, your grandfather built a real house. Can you show me how to make the bedroom walls stand up?"

"How do you want it to go?" Ali asked, looking at the jumble of wood.

Tess's face lit up. "I want one big living room

93

and then a cozy little bedroom at the back," Tess said. "Maybe we could put a roof on the bedroom and have stairs going up to it, and that could be his second-floor den."

"You're crazy," Ali said, laughing. "Rabbits don't go up stairs."

"A ramp, then," Tess said. "We could build a ramp."

"Let's just concentrate on building the big room first," Ali said. "Then we can put the bedroom inside it and then we'll put the roof on."

"Okay," Tess said excitedly. "I can hardly wait. Look, Rajah, this is going to be your house. You'll be able to go in your bedroom when Max starts playing the piano too loudly!"

As they worked together on the rabbit house, sometimes hitting fingers instead of nails, Ali forgot that she had been so mad at Tess.

"One day I might even start my own zoo," Tess said. "I'd specialize in endangered species, of course. So this cage-building experience will be good for me."

"I thought you wanted to join a circus," Ali said.

"I do," Tess said. "But later, when I'm rich, then I'd like to start saving endangered species. What about you—what do you want to do?"

"I have no idea," Ali said.

Tess grinned. "I tell you one thing you'd better not be."

"What's that?"

"A movie critic! Think of all the movies you couldn't watch because you were scared of them."

Ali laughed, but inside she felt mad again. Was Tess going to keep finding ways to put her down? Ali shivered. The wind off the ocean was cold and blustery. Raindrops peppered the porch roof and a tile flapped, reminding Ali of last night's ghost. She looked out over the dunes. Sand was blowing in fine clouds across the beach, and only seabirds stood at the edge of the fierce waves. Ali's gaze swept around until it came to rest on the point. An old rotting boathouse jutted out over the water. When she had been little, Josh had scared her once in that boathouse. She had been exploring with Mandy Johnson, and Josh had followed them and made spooky noises. Seeing it now gave Ali an idea to get back at Tess. "I just remembered that there really is one ghost in Rose Bay," Ali said casually.

"No kidding. Where?"

"See that old boathouse?" Alison said, pointing at it. "Well, an old man drowned there once, and people say they've seen strange lights and heard strange noises there."

"Really?" Tess asked, her eyes open very wide. "Has anyone actually seen this ghost?"

"I don't know," Alison said. "I've only heard about the lights and noises. I don't think anyone wanted to hang around long enough to see it. I thought you might want to check it out."

"Now?"

"Now's no good," Alison said. "It has to be dark. You wouldn't see the lights in the daytime."

"Oh, right," Tess said. She swallowed. "You want to take a look tonight, then? We'd have to sneak out. Your mom would never let you go!"

This was a point Alison had overlooked. She wanted to give Tess a good scare, but it had to be dark to be effective, and, as Tess had said, she would never be allowed to wander around in the dark. "That's a problem," she said.

"You could sleep over at my house," Tess said. "Then nobody would stop us."

"Good idea," Alison agreed. "I'll try to persuade my mom to let me."

Ali spent the rest of the morning thinking of the right thing to say to her mother. By the time she went home for tea, she had come up with a perfect scheme.

"Tess wants me to sleep over at her house," she said.

"Oh, Alison, I don't think . . . ," her mother began, as Ali knew she would.

"It was nice of Tess's mother to invite me back," Ali said quickly. "It might be rude if you said no after she let Tess sleep here."

Ali knew that her mother tried never to be rude. "I wouldn't want it to seem that I was snubbing them," she said, "but I do expect you to go to bed early."

"Don't worry, Mom," Alison said and left it at that.

Right after supper, she carried her sleeping bag over to Tess's house.

"I can't believe she agreed," Tess greeted her excitedly. "It's a miracle."

"I promised I wouldn't stay up too late," Ali said.

"That's okay. The ghost will come out as soon as it gets dark, won't he?" Tess asked.

Even though she was supposed to be the one scaring Tess, Ali's heart was beating very fast when they slipped downstairs after nine and crept out the back door. Tess was pretty sure her own parents would have let her go out in the dark, but somehow it made it more fun to slip out past them. They were both reading in the living room. Max's Sunday paper was spread all over the floor and Maggie was sitting neatly against the far wall, Indian-style, her hair spilling over the pages of a paperback. Neither one of them looked up.

"So far, so good," Tess whispered.

It was totally dark when the girls finally reached the point. The stars and moon were hidden by heavy clouds, and the wind was strong and cold. They had brought a flashlight, but its beam cut only a tiny circle of light into the darkness.

"Are you sure we haven't already passed it?" Tess whispered.

"There it is," Alison answered, shining the flashlight toward the black square in the distance.

"Turn the light out," Tess said. "We won't see the ghost's light if ours is shining."

Alison clicked off the light, and the night closed around them. "We'll turn it on again when we go inside," Tess whispered.

The wind had now dropped, and Alison was conscious of the sound their feet made as they shuffled through the sand. She could hear the loud crash of the waves along the shore.

When she had thought this whole adventure through in broad daylight, Alison had planned to lure Tess into the house, then scare her by flashing lights, making moaning noises, or tapping on the wall. But now, in the darkness, Ali felt too scared herself to go through with her plan.

"Do you want to go in?" Tess asked, pausing outside the door.

"If you do."

"I guess so."

"Okay, but go slowly. I have to turn the light on again," Alison said. "There's no floor in a boathouse—that's how the old man drowned in the first place. There are just boards around the edge."

"Okay," Tess said. She lifted the latch, and the door opened with a creek. Cold, damp air mingled with the smell of rotting wood came out to meet them. Tess hesitated. Then she took the flashlight from Ali and swung it around the boathouse, taking in the pulleys that once lowered the boats and the cobweb-covered beams across the roof.

"Boy, it really is spooky in here," she said, and her voice echoed.

She continued to shine the flashlight around the walls until it touched on a pile of rags in the corner.

"Ali, did you see that?" Tess whispered, her voice high and tight now.

"What?"

"Those rags. I thought they moved. Did you see them move?"

Before Ali could answer, there came a low moan from the corner. Tess grabbed Ali. The flashlight swung violently, sending light dancing from the rafters to the black water beneath. The pile of rags rose up from the shadowy corner, slowly taking the shape of a terrible old man with sunken eyes and matted hair. He gave another moan and started to come toward them. "Go away!" he croaked in a scratchy voice.

The girls fought each other for the door. Alison managed to get out first, but Tess pushed past her, the flashlight falling from her hand as she collided with Alison. There were sounds behind them; grunts and unearthly shouts echoed through the boathouse.

"Quick, run," Tess yelled, taking off like a young deer, bounding over the scrub. Alison ran as fast as she could, too, not daring to look over her shoulder. Her heart was hammering inside her chest, and her breath came in gulps. She commanded her legs to go faster. Tess was a light shape in the darkness ahead of her. She jumped over a clump of bushes, felt the scratch of thorns, landed with her foot in a rabbit hole, and went down hard, sprawling on the sandy path.

She lay there, too frightened to cry out. She waited to feel icy hands grab her, the terrible old man taking her with him to the land of the dead. Tess would never even know what happened. She'd just keep running and arrive home with no Alison. By the time anyone came looking for her, it would be too late. . . .

Suddenly, hands *were* grabbing her, but they were warm and small, and Tess's voice was in her ear. "Come on, Ali, get up. Here, take my hand. Are you okay?"

"I think I twisted my ankle." Ali panted, clinging to Tess's outstretched hand like a lifeline.

"Come on, Ali, we have to get out of here," Tess coaxed, half dragging Alison, her arm firmly around her as they stumbled forward.

"Is he still coming after us?" Alison managed to ask.

"I don't think so," Tess panted back. "Let's keep going, just in case."

They lurched on, arms around each other.

"Tess, I've got to stop. My foot's killing me," Ali said.

They paused, gasping and panting, looking at each other as if amazed they were both still alive.

"I've never been so scared, have you?" Tess gasped, "I mean, what was that? Do you think it was a real ghost?"

"I don't know," Ali said.

"And then *you* scared me," Tess said. "I turned around, and you weren't there. I didn't know where you were. I thought I'd have to go back into that awful place to find you."

"You came back for me!" Ali said in awe. "I thought you'd gone on without me."

"Would I do that?" Tess demanded. "Friends don't leave friends to be taken by ghosts. . . ."

They looked at each other, and Alison could see Tess grinning in the darkness.

"Thanks, Tess," she said, feeling dangerously near tears.

"How's your ankle?" Tess asked. "Do you think you can make it home?"

"I think so."

"Come on, then," Tess said, slipping her arm around Alison. "Lean on me."

"Okay," Alison said, feeling the warmth of Tess's arm across her cold back.

"Hey, Ali?" Tess asked as they met up with the path along the shore. "You know what?"

"What?"

"Let's not go ghost hunting again, okay?"

"Okay," Ali said. She wrapped her own arm around Tess's shoulders, leaning on Tess as she limped toward the lights of home.

Chapter 12

Alison's ankle was hurting badly by the time they made it back to Tess's house, but she pretended it wasn't.

"Do you think a doctor should take a look at it, Ali?" Tess asked. "It's swollen already."

"It's fine," Ali said. "It doesn't hurt much anymore."

She felt comforted by Tess's presence right now. Besides, if she called her mother, her mother would want to know how she hurt her ankle, and she didn't feel strong enough to think up a good story yet. As she lay on the pillows on Tess's floor, her foot throbbing as if an elephant was doing trampoline exercises on it, she decided she would never, ever recount those moments of terror again for anyone.

"Do you think we imagined it?" she whispered to Tess.

"Do you?" Tess asked.

"No," Ali said. "I don't think I could imagine anything as horrible as that."

"Me either," Tess said. "Do you think it really was a ghost?"

"What else could it have been?"

"I don't know. Maybe there's a perfectly good explanation for it," Tess said.

"Let's not talk about it anymore," Ali suggested.

"Good idea," Tess said. "Let's forget it ever happened, okay?"

"Okay," Ali said.

By the next morning, her ankle was very swollen and it hurt her to put any weight on it. There was no question of hiding it anymore. Maggie phoned Ali's house, and Grandpa came to get her in the car.

"I twisted it in a rabbit hole," she told her mother. "We were having a race."

"Oh, Ali," her mother said, shaking her head. "When did this happen?"

"Just a little while ago," Ali said evasively.

"It looks serious," her mother said, prodding at it gently. "I don't like that swelling. I just hope it's not broken. We'd better drive you straight to Dr. Graham."

Ali tried to argue, but she was packed into the car and off to the doctor's office.

It was midmorning before Grandpa carried her into the house again and installed her, with an ice pack on her ankle, on the big wicker sofa out in the conservatory, which was the name her grandparents gave to the glassed-in porch facing the ocean. Everyone made a big fuss over her. Her mother propped her up with pillows and tucked a blanket around her, even though it wasn't cold. Grandpa fixed up a little table so that she could do a jigsaw puzzle, and Grandma baked her favorite gingerbread cookies. Robbie came and sat at her feet with a sad expression on his face.

"How will you walk to school with only one foot, Ali?" he asked.

"It will be better by the time school starts," Ali said.

"It will?" Robbie asked, still looking scared. "You won't have to have your foot cut off, will you?" he asked.

Ali laughed. "Of course not. It's only a sprain. I didn't even break it," she said.

Robbie got up, relieved. "That's good," he said. "Josh said you'd probably have to have your foot chopped off, maybe your whole leg."

"Josh was just teasing," Ali said. She was glad that Josh was making fun of her injuries. The way the others were hovering around her with looks of concern and sympathy made her feel guilty, especially when she thought of how she had hurt her foot doing something sneaky. The doctor had given her a pain pill, which made her sleepy. The moment she closed her eyes, she saw the moan-

105

ing figure from the boathouse coming toward her.

She was very glad when Tess showed up.

"Are you okay?" Tess asked. "What did the doctor say?"

Ali made a face. "He said it's sprained."

"That's good, right?"

"Not too great," Ali said. "He said that sprains sometimes take longer to heal than breaks and that it might be several weeks before I can walk on it."

"Several weeks! That's terrible," Tess said. "What will I do without you?" She sat down on the edge of the sofa. "I guess I'll just have to entertain you. So, what do you want to do? Play a game of cards?"

Ali looked out of the window. Josh was running toward the ocean with Robbie behind him. She looked back at Tess. "You don't have to hang around indoors with me," she said. "I'll be fine."

Tess got to her feet. "Okay. See you in three weeks." She started to walk toward the door, then turned back and laughed. "You goob," she said. "You didn't think I'd really walk out on you, did you? I've got to take good care of you so that your foot gets better as quickly as possible. There's so much we haven't done yet this summer. We've got to go to the water-slide park and the boardwalk in Southhaven, and I've got to learn to snorkel so we can visit the octopus. Max was even talking about renting a sailboat."

"Your dad?" Ali couldn't imagine Max, the musical genius, in a sailboat.

"He used to sail when he was a kid," Tess said. "He wants me to have a good time here."

"Well," Ali said. "You can go sailing without me. You'll have fun with your parents."

"Yeah, sure," Tess said, looking away, and lifting her hair off her shoulders nervously. "Maggie would never come with us."

"Why? Doesn't she like the ocean?" Ali asked.

"She likes to paint it," Tess said. "But that's about it. That's all that seems to matter to her these days—her painting, I mean. She might not even . . ." She broke off and paused for a minute. "Hey, I almost forgot about the carnival. Your foot has to be better in time for us to go on all those rides. It'll be here the middle of August, right? That's a whole month away. Your foot has to be better by then."

"I hope so," Ali said. "I'll go crazy if I have to sit here and have everyone fuss over me for a whole month! Grandma will feed me until I'm fat as a blimp, and my mom will examine my toes every two seconds to see if infection is setting in." She laughed, then stopped when she saw the sad look on Tess's face. It was that faraway look again. Ali wanted to ask Tess what was happening with her family. She wondered if Max and Maggie were still fighting. She knew Tess would never talk about it, though, so she quickly changed the subject.

"I'll be well for the carnival, no matter what," she said. "Even if I have to hop around on one foot, nothing will stop us."

"Tell me about the rides," Tess said. "Do they have the Scream Machine, the one that turns completely upside down?"

"I don't think so," Alison said. "But they have the Tilt-a-Whirl and the Flying Bobs that go backwards, and a Gravitron—you know, it spins so fast the floor drops away and you stick to the wall."

"Cool," Tess said. "I've never been on one of those. We'll go on every ride and we'll make ourselves sick eating hot dogs and cotton candy and caramel apples and pretzels, okay?"

"Okay," Alison said, feeling pure happiness as she imagined it. "And don't forget the saltwater taffy. And the Haunted House."

The next two days, Tess came over to Ali's house in the morning and stayed with her all day. They played long games of Monopoly and had competitions to see who could build the biggest house of cards.

On the third morning, Grandpa carried Ali out onto the lawn. Tess brought Rajah over and showed Ali his new tricks. Having a sprained ankle wasn't so bad after all, Ali decided. She was having a great time.

But the following morning, Tess did not show up. Alison lay on the wicker sofa and worried, peering over the shrubs every five minutes to see if Tess was coming.

"Where can she be?" she asked her mother when she brought lunch in on a tray.

"Honey, maybe she wanted a day to herself," her mother said gently. "You two have been seeing an awful lot of each other. I'm sure her family just decided to go somewhere for the day and she'll call you as soon as she gets back."

So Alison could do nothing but sit and worry. She worried that something had happened to Tess, or that Tess found it boring sitting inside all day when she could be on a beach.

The day seemed long and empty. Ali looked at her games and books, and none of them seemed interesting enough to bother with. She realized she had gotten used to Tess saying, "Let's do this or let's go there."

That evening she called Tess. The phone rang and rang, but nobody answered.

The next morning, just as Ali was prepared to spend another day bored and alone, she heard light footsteps tapping down the stone hallway.

"Sorry about yesterday," Tess said, appearing

in the sun-porch doorway. "I was going to call, but I didn't get around to it."

Alison looked at her. There was something different about her today.

"What's up?" Ali asked.

"Why?"

"You look . . . um . . . tired."

Tess put her hands into her shorts pockets. "I had a tiring day yesterday, I guess," she said.

"Doing what?"

"Packing," Tess said with a casual shrug. "I had to help Maggie pack her things." She paused and kicked the edge of the rug.

"She's going somewhere?"

"Yeah." Tess kicked the rug again. "An art show," she said at last. "She's got an art show in Florida. Miami, I think."

"Did you drive her to the airport?"

Tess shook her head. "She took a taxi."

There was a silence. The clock on the shelf ticked away noisily.

"So you and your dad are alone?" Alison asked.

"Yeah, but we'll be fine," Tess said quickly. "We're a great team, Max and I." She hunched her shoulders as she drove her hands deeper into her pockets.

"You can eat here as often as you want," she said. "My grandmother loves having you, because you enjoy her cooking so much."

Tess nodded seriously. "Well, I have to go," she said. "I just came over so you wouldn't think I'd forgotten you. I have to go into town with Max today. See you tomorrow, okay?"

"Sure, see you tomorrow," Alison said uneasily. She watched Tess go back across the lawn, plodding heavily, as if she carried a great weight on her shoulders.

Chapter 13

Two weeks after their adventure at the boathouse, Ali's ankle was strong enough to walk on again. Her mother warned her not to do too much too quickly, but at least she could go down to the beach with Tess without being carried. Tess wanted to practice using the snorkel and mask so that she could find the octopus. Ali lay in the sand on the raft and gave instructions while various parts of Tess appeared above the water.

"Ali," Tess yelled, her face appearing suddenly in front of the raft. "I think I saw something. It's white and wiggly. Do you think it's a baby octopus? Oh, no, it's my foot!" Then she collapsed into helpless laughter.

"It's a good thing you weren't spearfishing," Ali commented, making Tess laugh even harder. She slid off her raft. "Want to go for a swim now?" she asked. "The doctor says I need to swim to strengthen my ankle."

"Let's go, then," Tess said, flinging her mask onto the sand. "We have to get you back in

112

shape. Max promised to drive us into Southhaven when your mom says it's okay. He's going to treat us to the water slides and everything!"

"That's great," Ali said, wading knee-deep into the water. "It sounds as though you two are getting along pretty well."

Tess nodded. "He's been trying hard," she said. "He wants to make the summer fun for me. He asked me what I'd like to do, and I said, go to Southhaven with Ali."

A few days later, Ali's mother agreed that she was strong enough to go with Tess to Southhaven. Ali was really looking forward to a day with Tess, but she wasn't so sure about a whole day with Max. She was still scared of his temper. But as they started out on a perfect sunny morning, Ali could tell that Max was trying hard to be nice. He let them turn the car radio to a rock station and then sang along with them to all the songs, making funny faces out of the car window when other people noticed the loud blast of music.

When they got to the water-slide park, he settled himself under a tree with the morning paper. There were four slides, three that came down in gentle spirals through tunnels, and one, called Niagara Falls, that plunged straight down in four incredible drops. After the girls had tried the other three, Tess suggested Niagara Falls.

"I will if you will," Ali said.

"You want to go first?" Tess asked.

"No way. You go first," Ali answered.

"Let's go together," Tess said. "That way we'll die at the same time."

Ali climbed onto the mat behind Tess and clung tightly to her waist. One minute the mat was inching forward, and the next they were hurtling downward. Ali tried to scream, but no sound came out. They poised for a second at the next fall, then plunged downward again. Ali closed her eyes tightly. She felt as if her stomach were still somewhere up at the top. Suddenly, they splashed into cold water. Ali went under, and water flew up her nose and into her eyes. Strong hands grabbed at her and lifted her up.

"You two okay?" a deep, male voice asked. Before they could answer, the most gorgeous lifeguard Tess and Ali had ever seen helped them to their feet. "It's a shock the first time, isn't it?" he asked and winked at them.

Gasping, they staggered to the side of the pool and got out.

"That was scary!" Tess panted.

Ali nodded. "I left my stomach behind."

"And that cold water at the bottom. I thought my heart was going to stop."

"Me too!"

"That lifeguard was really cute! Did you see his long eyelashes?"

Ali nodded. "My heart almost stopped again when I looked up and saw him!"

Tess looked up at the steep slide, then back at the guard in the pool. "Want to go on it again?"

"Yeah!" Ali said.

"How are the slides, girls?" Max asked later, when they were both cold and breathless from several trips down Niagara Falls.

"Great. You ought to try one," Tess said. "Niagara's the best. Right, Ali?"

"Yeah, it's fun," Ali said.

Max nodded and stood up. The girls watched him climb to the top of the slide, then come hurtling down, yelling and waving his arms, with a look of terror on his face.

"Fun?" he demanded, staggering out of the pool. "You kids are monsters. That's enough fun for one day. I need some lunch to steady my nerves."

They drove into Southhaven and parked by the boardwalk, which ran the length of the beach. It was lined with booths and kiddie rides on the side away from the ocean. On a weekday afternoon it was not crowded, but noisy from the sounds of the merry-go-round and the sideshow barkers trying to get customers. Scraps of litter blew around, and sea gulls fought for pieces of dropped food.

Max spied a hot-dog cart. "Ah, Polish dogs. Perfect." He ordered his with sauerkraut and extra onions.

"That's so gross, Max," Tess said, looking at the heap on top of the sausage.

"You should try it. It's good," Max said. "I always ate these at the boardwalk when I was a kid."

So they both ordered one. After one bite, Tess made a terrible face at Ali and they both scraped off the sauerkraut.

"The onions are good, though," Tess admitted.

Ali nodded, then grinned as she thought of something. "We should buy a postcard to send to your mother and describe what we're eating. She'd have a fit!" she said, laughing.

Tess did not laugh. "She probably wouldn't care," she said. "She's too busy with her art show."

"Have you heard from her?" Ali asked.

"I got a postcard," she said, "with palm trees on it."

"Did she say when she's coming back?" Ali asked.

Tess seemed to be very interested in her hot dog. "She didn't say."

"You must miss her," Ali said sympathetically.

"I do not!" Tess said loudly.

"I—I just thought," Ali stammered. "I mean, when she first went away, I thought . . ."

"I'm not like you, you know," Tess said airily. "I'm not used to having a mother fussing over me all the time like yours does. Max and I are doing great. Right, Max?"

Max turned around. "What?"

"I said we make a great team, right?"

Max put an arm around her shoulder. "You bet," he said. "So how was the kraut dog?"

"The dog was fine. The kraut was disgusting," Tess said. "We need something to take the taste away."

"Like what?" Max asked.

"One of those big waffle cones with two scoops of ice cream and lots of hot fudge and whipped cream on top."

"You're not serious," Max said.

"Of course I am," Tess said. "Ali wants one, too, don't you, Ali?"

"Maybe later," Ali said, holding her stomach.

"Later is right," Max said. "I don't want you two throwing up on the way home. Right now I need a cup of coffee."

"Ali and I will go explore," Tess said. "Can we have some money?"

Max sighed. "She thinks I'm made of money," he said, but he handed over a five-dollar bill.

"Come on, Al, let's live," Tess said, dragging

117

Ali down the boardwalk toward the game booths. They played and lost two games before Tess started thinking about food again. "Hey, look," she yelled excitedly. "There's the place that sells the waffle cones. Doesn't it smell good?"

Ali shuddered. "Don't," she said. "I'm still too full of hot dog to think about ice cream."

Tess grinned. "Better toughen up that stomach before the carnival, or you won't be able to keep up with me. I plan to eat everything, and I mean everything: cotton candy and caramel apples and pretzels and hot dogs and—"

"I hope you have a ton of money if you're going to eat all that stuff," Ali interrupted. "They always charge so much at carnivals."

"I think Max will give me some money," Tess said, glancing back at him. "How about you?"

Ali made a face. "My parents give us each five dollars," she said, "which isn't nearly enough. All the best rides cost a dollar fifty!"

"What a rip-off!" Tess exclaimed. "Max will probably only give me ten dollars." She kicked a hot-dog bun so that it toppled off the boardwalk to the sand below, where it was pounced on by shrieking sea gulls. "It's a bummer not having any money, isn't it? I get an allowance, but it always seems to disappear."

"Me too," Ali said. "One movie and I've blown it."

Tess leaned over the railing, then noticed Max coming down the boardwalk toward them.

"So what now, ladies?" Max called to them. "Are you as tired and overstuffed as I am?" he asked hopefully.

"No way," Tess said, grabbing his arm. "We've got to try some of the midway games, and we've found the place that sells giant waffle cones."

Max looked ill. "Waffle cones?" he asked. "You're sure you want waffle cones?"

"Sure," Tess said. "We need dessert, right, Ali?" Tess asked.

"Do you think I'm made of money or something?" Max asked.

"If you sign that deal for the new musical, you'll be made of money," Tess said. "I heard you talking to your agent over the phone. A musical with Del Lindsay should make you millions!"

"Del Lindsay?" Ali repeated excitedly. "Tess, you didn't tell me it was definite."

"It's not," Max said. "It's still in the pipeline. I don't want to talk about it too soon. That's bad luck."

"So can we have waffle cones on the strength of maybe?" Tess asked.

Max looked at Alison. "Is my daughter such a pain when she's with you?" he asked. "Does she do nothing but nag and bully all the time?"

"All the time," Ali said, nudging Tess.

They each had a waffle cone with two scoops of ice cream and lots of chocolate syrup. Then they headed home.

That night, when Ali got into bed, she started to think about money again. In earlier summers, it hadn't mattered too much if she only had enough money for a couple of rides at the carnival, because she usually had to ride them alone anyway. But with Tess she wanted to try all the rides, all the games, and eat everything. Somehow she'd have to persuade her mother to give her more money this year.

While they were setting the table for lunch the next day, she brought up the subject.

"Will you be giving me money for the carnival this year?" she asked.

"I guess so, if you're good," her mother said, still concentrating on draining the water from green beans. "I gave you five dollars last year, didn't I?"

"But, Mom, five dollars isn't enough," Ali said. "Do you know how much the rides cost these days?"

Her mother looked up over the steam and smiled. "Then I guess we could make it six," she said.

"Six!" Ali wailed in despair.

"You get your allowance," Mrs. Hinkle said calmly. "You could save that for the carnival."

Ali sighed. "Mom, isn't there any job I could do around the house for money? I can't have a good time with six dollars."

Her mother smiled. "We all take our turns with chores in this family, as you very well know. Besides, you can't even keep your own room clean!"

Ali didn't say any more, but the question of money for the carnival came up again when Josh burst in after they were all seated for lunch.

"Guess what, everybody?" he demanded, sliding into his place. "Wait until you hear this." He looked around, grinning delightedly. "I've got a job!"

"A job? Where? Doing what?"

Josh looked as if he had just been elected president. "I've been hired to help set up the carnival and take it down again when it's over."

"Oh, Joshua," Mrs. Hinkle began. "You're not old enough for that sort of work yet."

"Aw, Mom," Josh began.

But Grandpa interrupted. "Won't hurt him one bit, Helen," he said. "I worked a couple of carnivals when I was a kid. Build some muscles on him."

"And I'm getting paid five bucks an hour, Grandpa," Josh said. "Think of all the carnival rides that will pay for! Of course, by the time they open, I'll probably know all the ride people, and maybe they'll let me on for free."

After lunch, Alison couldn't wait to tell Tess. She rode straight over to Tess's house.

"Guess what?" she called as she saw Tess outside cleaning out Rajah's new condo. "Josh got a job setting up the carnival. They pay five dollars an hour."

"Wow, five dollars an hour. I could use that," Tess said with a sigh. "Do you think we could get hired there?"

"I don't think so," Alison said. "You have to be fourteen to work."

Tess frowned. "We're too young for everything. I wish I could hurry and grow up."

Alison nodded. "I've been thinking of all the things I could do if only I had some money. Not just for the carnival . . ."

"I know what you mean," Tess said. "And I'm getting worried about asking Max. He's really tense about this musical and about . . . Well, he's really tense."

"You could mention it next time you write to your mother," Alison suggested. "Parents who are far away are more likely to cough it up."

Tess shook her head. "I can't do that," she said shortly. "We need to get a job."

"What could we do?"

"How about baby-sitting? I saw a lot of babies down at the beach."

"Most of the families here bring a mother's helper with them," Ali said.

"What else could we do at our age?"

"You could put on a circus. You're very good."

Tess poked a finger through the wire to stroke Rajah. "Not good enough yet. Someone might not understand that Rajah is a substitute lion and they might laugh. That would really hurt his feelings."

"So come up with another bright idea. You're the creative one," Alison said. "It will be terrible if the carnival comes and we can only go on a couple of rides. What if we don't even win one stuffed animal? Not that you need one," she added. "You already have a bed full."

"But I've always wanted a great big stuffed unicorn," Tess said with a sigh. "We'll just have to find a way to make money. You want to ride into Rose Bay and study the ads on the board at the store?"

"Sure," Alison said, not too hopefully. "I don't know what we'll find there, though. They usually only advertise for crew members for fishing boats."

"Maybe today will be different," Tess said. "Come on, I know we'll find something. I think it's our lucky day."

Chapter 14

Half an hour later they were standing outside Coby's Bait, Tackle, and General Store, taking in the fishy smell of bait mingling with the warm, caramelly smell of saltwater taffy being pulled at the machine in the window. They each bought some, falling into silence as they chewed and studied the notice board in the corner. As Alison had predicted, there were a couple of notices for deckhands and one for a racing crew member. There were also a couple for housecleaning. Then Tess spied a little notice at the bottom of the board and started flapping her arms wildly, making squawking noises as she fought to clear her mouth of the taffy.

She grabbed Alison's arm and pointed. "Look," she managed to say at last. "They want a cat-sitter! That's the most perfect job in the world for me. Cats are like little lions. Maybe I can practice my training while I cat-sit. Where's Piney Drive? I can't wait!"

"That's great for you, but what about me?" Alison asked grudgingly.

"Oh," Tess said, turning to Alison as if she had forgotten that Alison existed. She glanced up at the board. "Well, there's nothing for you here, unless you want to clean houses. But you can ask your family. They know everyone around here. I'm sure they know someone who'll give you a job."

"My mom's already reminded me that I can't even keep my own room clean," she said.

"Don't worry about it," Tess said. "Maybe it will be a long cat-sit and I'll make enough money for both of us."

Alison wanted to say that it wouldn't be the same and that she couldn't take Tess's money, but she didn't think she could say anything without getting angry at Tess.

"I guess I'd better go over to Piney Drive," Tess said after a minute.

"Okay," Ali said. "See you later."

Tess smiled. "Yeah, see you later, after I'm hired as official cat-sitter! I hope he's the sort of cat that can jump through hoops."

Alison rode home alone, feeling hurt and angry. *What kind of friend is Tess?* she asked herself. Weren't friends supposed to share everything? Weren't they supposed to do things together? At school she always went along with what the others wanted. She had thought it would be different with Tess. *I always let her get her own way,* she realized. She knew that Tess was not trying to be mean. She just didn't know how to share.

Ali was about to sit down for family tea when there was a tap at the kitchen window and Tess beckoned her furiously outside. She slipped out to find Tess red-faced and excited. "Guess what?" she asked. "I think I've got the job."

"That's great," Alison said weakly.

"They're giving me a couple of days' trial," Tess said. "They go away on Saturday and they want to make sure Mr. Purr is happy."

"Mr. Purr?"

"He's a big old Persian," Tess said. "He's very sweet. Want to see him?" She pointed to the big wicker basket on the ground beside her.

"You've got him with you?" Alison asked. "Does looking after him include taking him on walks?"

Tess giggled. "No, dummy," she said. "I'm taking him home. They want me to cat-sit at my house because they're subletting theirs."

"But, Tess," Alison said in disbelief. "Your dad is allergic to animals. What will you do?"

Tess tossed her hair back airily. "I'll keep him in my bedroom," she said. "Max never goes in there, and Mr. Purr isn't the kind of cat who wanders. I'll keep his litter box in my closet. He should be just fine. It's only for two weeks."

"I don't know, Tess," Alison said. "How can you keep a cat in a room for two weeks?"

"Easy," Tess said. "I'll just stay in my room and keep him company. You can come over and visit me all the time. We'll try training him when he's settled in." She bent to pick up the basket. "He's awfully heavy," she said. "Could you give me a hand?"

"We're just about to eat," Alison said.

"Oh." Tess looked disappointed, as if Ali had let her down.

"Do you want to come over and spend the night?" she asked. "Just to make sure he's going to be okay?"

Alison wanted to say that Mr. Purr was Tess's problem, but Tess turned her big, dark eyes on Ali. "Please . . . pretty please?" she asked. "Pretty please with sugar on top."

Alison laughed and gave Tess a little push. "Oh, go away," she said. "I'll come over if I can."

Ali's mother agreed reluctantly. "Just don't have any more races over sand dunes," she said. "If you hurt your ankle again, you'll miss the carnival."

"Don't worry, we plan to stay in Tess's room all evening," Alison said, glad that she didn't have to lie. She had almost hoped her mother would forbid her to spend the night and that Tess would have a terrible time alone with Mr. Purr.

Tess greeted her with a big grin and a finger to her lips. "Max didn't notice a thing," she whispered. "I just walked straight past him and up to my room with Mr. Purr. This is going to be a snap."

She opened her door cautiously. "See, he loves it already," she said, pointing to a big white fluffy cat draped on her bed. It was almost indistinguishable from Tess's pile of stuffed animals. "If Max ever looks in here, he won't even notice," she said, closing the door behind her. "Mr. Purr is a real sweetie, aren't you, honey pie?"

She picked him up to hug him. Mr. Purr lay in her arms, still looking just like a stuffed animal. "I don't know about the lion training, though," she said, shaking her head sadly. "I don't think he can stay awake long enough."

She put the cat back on her bed and the girls settled down to a game of cards. About ten o'clock Mr. Purr woke up, stretched, looked around, and realized he was in a strange room. He opened his mouth and gave a very loud *MIAUUUUW!* Tess leaped up. "Quick, sing," she commanded. Ali began, "Row, row, row your boat," at the same time as Tess began, "She loves you, yeah, yeah yeah."

"Keep it down up there," came Max's voice from below. "That's a horrible noise you're making."

Tess and Ali put their hands to their mouths, trying to stifle their nervous laughter. Luckily, Mr. Purr had looked around in horror at the sudden loud noise and had taken refuge in the closet.

"I've got a bad feeling about this," Ali whispered. "I don't think it's going to work."

"Of course it will work," Tess said. "If we get through tonight and Max doesn't get sick, he'll let me keep the cat anyway."

The cat appeared from the closet again and began slinking around the room.

"Looks like he wants out," Ali whispered.

"He'll get used to it, won't you, baby," Tess crooned. She picked him up and put him on her lap. Around eleven they gave the cat some food and went to bed. Mr. Purr came and curled up next to Tess. "What did I tell you?" she asked happily. "He'll just love it here."

In the middle of the night, Ali woke to find something scrabbling and snuffling close to her face. It sounded like a large animal, and for a second she wondered whether Mr. Purr was gentle by day and a killer by night. She sat up.

"It's only me," Tess whispered.

"What are you doing?" Ali whispered back.

"Don't get upset, but I think I've lost Mr.

Purr," Tess whispered. "I was checking to see if he was on your sleeping bag."

"He isn't."

"Then he's lost."

"He can't be. The door's closed. He's hiding."

"Just one small thing," Tess said. "I got up to get a drink of water. I only had the door open for a minute. Come on, we've got to find him."

"You find him. You're the official cat-sitter. I'm sleepy," Alison mumbled, already lying down again.

"Ali, please? I'm doomed if Max finds him. I'll never get another chance to make money, and I'll never win a stuffed unicorn in my entire life. Please?"

Alison got out of her warm sleeping bag. The night felt cold. She followed Tess along the hall. Tess looked back over her shoulder. "One good thing," she whispered. "He can't be in Max's room. He always sleeps with the door closed. . . ." Her voice died away as she noticed Max's wide-open door.

"You don't think . . ." Tess whispered.

The sound of a big sneeze came from Max's direction.

"Oh, no," Tess gasped. "Come on."

Ali decided that waking a sleeping Max with a cat near him was about as appealing as trying to take the goose with the golden egg away from a sleeping giant, but she followed Tess into the darkness of the big master bedroom. Max was lying diagonally across the bed, one arm thrown out from the covers. There, nestled in the curve of Max's arm, was Mr. Purr. He looked very pleased with himself.

Tess glanced at Ali. "I'll lift his arm. You grab the cat and run for it, okay?" she whispered.

Gently, Tess took hold of Max's pajama sleeve and moved his arm inch by inch. "Now," she hissed.

Ali slipped her hands around Mr. Purr and pulled. "He doesn't want to come. He's dug in his claws," Ali whispered as the entire blanket threatened to come up with the cat. Tess rushed to Ali's aid and pried the claws loose one by one. Mr. Purr gave a protesting yowl. Max rolled over, opened his eyes, and sneezed loudly. Ali gasped and stepped back with the cat into the shadow of the door. Max focused on Tess. "What are you doing?" he asked.

"I heard you sneezing," Tess said sweetly. "I wondered if you were sick or something."

Ali stifled the nervous giggle that threatened to break out any second.

"Sweet of you, punkin," Max said. "Come to think of it, I do feel strange—all itchy, and my eyes are running."

"Twenty-four-hour bug," Tess said quickly. "I hear it's going around."

"I hope it clears up in twenty-four hours," Max said. "I hate getting sick."

"I guarantee it will be gone in the morning," Tess said. "Would you like some tea or something?"

"I think I'll just try to sleep it off," Max said.

He rolled over, and Tess melted into the shadows to join Ali. "Don't say it," she hissed as they reached the safety of her room. "I know. The cat goes back in the morning." She reached out and fondled Mr. Purr. "It was a great idea while it lasted, wasn't it?"

Chapter 15

"Want to go for a bike ride into Rose Bay?" Ali asked Tess the next morning, once Mr. Purr had been returned to his owners.

"Sure," Tess said. "Maybe we could stop off on the way and rob a bank."

When they reached Rose Bay they saw flags being put up across the street in preparation for the carnival parade. The first trailers were parked in the big field where the rides would be, behind the swimming pool. Ali stopped to look at the carnival poster in the store window. Her eyes skimmed down the page until she spotted something near the bottom.

"Hey, look at this! I don't believe it!" She shouted.

Tess came over. "What?"

Ali was waving her finger excitedly at the page. "Look. It says, 'Cash prizes for parade entries.'"

"How much?"

"It doesn't say. They never gave money before."

"What if it's a hundred dollars," Tess said.

Ali's heart beat faster. "A hundred dollars? It couldn't be that much, could it?"

Tess studied the poster. "What category could we enter?" she asked. "We don't have horses. We couldn't build a float, could we?"

"They have decorated bicycles for kids," Alison said. "There aren't too many entries, and they're usually not so great. One of us would have a good chance of winning."

"I have the greatest idea for decorating my bike!" Tess said, looking at Ali excitedly. "I bet nobody has done it before."

"What?" Alison asked, still bubbling with excitement.

"You'll see," Tess said, tossing her hair mysteriously. "I'm going right home to start working on it. Boy, is it going to be terrific. I can't wait."

She jumped on her bike and started to pedal away.

"Hey, I saw the poster first," Ali yelled after Tess. "It was my idea. I told you about the decorated bikes." But Tess was already too far away to hear.

Ali biked slowly home. *I should never have told her*, she thought. *She'll probably win. How can I ever think of an idea as great as Tess's?*

She pushed the pedals harder and harder. *If I had come up with the great idea, we could have worked on it together,* she thought to herself. *But if that's how Tess wants it, I'll show her. I'll come up with a great idea, too. She'll be surprised when she sees she isn't the only one who can come up with a fantastic idea!*

The trouble was that no fantastic idea came to her. She wheeled her bike into the shed and studied it. It was sleek and elegant. There wasn't much of it to decorate. Her old bike was in the corner, with its flowery basket and upturned handlebars. She picked it up and started to wheel it around, hoping for inspiration. There was so much clutter in the shed. Everything the Hinkles had discarded for the past fifty years was stacked around the walls. Then Ali noticed an old baby buggy in the corner, and an idea began to form. The old-fashioned, high wheels looked as if they belonged on an old horse-drawn carriage. If only she could find some way of attaching them to her bike. She could see clearly in her mind the effect she wanted: her bicycle as the horse, pulling an old-fashioned buggy, maybe with flowers around it. All the stuff was here, if only she could come up with a way of putting it together.

"It would never work," she told herself.

But at dinner that night, she was still thinking so hard that she hardly said a word.

"Alison, Grandpa asked you to pass the rolls," her mother said.

"Sorry, Grandpa. I didn't hear you," Ali said, handing them to him.

"You look like you've got the problems of the world on your shoulders," Grandpa said gently. "Come on, cheer up. A worry shared is a worry halved. What's the problem?"

Alison played with her fork. "It's the carnival parade, Grandpa," she said. "Tess and I are both entering the bicycle contest, and I know hers is going to be so good. I'm worried mine will look terrible next to hers."

"Don't enter if it's going to upset you," her mother said.

"But I want to enter. They're giving cash prizes this year," Alison said. "And I even have a good idea. I'm just not sure how to do it."

"Then why don't you tell us about it?" Grandpa suggested. "Maybe we'll be able to help."

Alison flushed. "Well, I was thinking . . . there's that old baby buggy in the shed."

Josh let out a laugh. "Alison as a baby. Sounds perfect."

"Be quiet, Josh. Go on, Alison," Grandpa said, giving him a frown.

"I was thinking maybe I could use the wheels from the buggy and make the bicycle into a little horse pulling a cart full of flowers," Alison explained.

"What a nice idea," Grandma said. "I can just picture it. I'm terrific at paper roses, remember?"

"Wow, Grandma, would you show me how?" Alison asked. "I could even dress up in old-fashioned clothes from the attic."

"And Grandpa and I can help with the wheels and stuff. Right, Grandpa?" Josh chimed in.

"Ali should do the actual putting together herself," her mother added. "It is her project."

"I will, I will," Alison said happily.

The next day when she saw Tess she was as mysterious about her project as Tess had been.

"You should see my bike," Tess said. "It's going to look so good."

"So's mine," Alison said.

Tess looked at her suspiciously. "I'll tell you what mine is if you tell me yours."

Alison considered. Tess couldn't copy hers even if she wanted to. "Okay," she said.

"Mine's going to be a dragon," Tess whispered. "When I was little, I used to pretend I was riding a dragon when I rode my bike. So I'm turning my bike into a big, fire-breathing dragon."

"Wow," Alison said. "That sounds great. You might win."

"How about yours?" Tess asked.

"Oh, I'm just going to pull a cart of flowers," Alison said.

"That will be pretty," Tess answered. Alison could tell by her face that Tess didn't think it was such a great idea. She grinned to herself when she thought of the costume and the old buggy wheels. Wouldn't Tess be surprised.

Everyone at Alison's house became very excited about her entry. Alison loved being the center of attention and loved thinking about how wonderful her bike would look. As it came together, it was even better than she had hoped. Josh had found an old hobbyhorse in the attic and they had managed to attach its head to the handlebars. Grandma had helped Alison put together a pretty blue and white outfit with big puffed sleeves and a lacy apron. When Alison studied herself in the mirror, she knew she looked pretty.

During the days before the carnival arrived, Ali saw very little of Tess. Tess was working hard on her own project and didn't want Alison to see it until the day of the parade. Whenever Ali did see Tess, Tess seemed grouchy and short-tempered. She admitted that her project was harder than she thought it would be. Ali realized that, as much as she loved her project, she wished she and Tess had worked together. She thought of how much fun they would have had making paper flowers.

August fifteenth was the opening of the carnival and the day of the big parade. Ali rode her bike into Rose Bay early. The town was bustling. People on horses and bikes were milling around, waiting to get in place for the parade. Cars honked, children screamed, dogs barked. There was no sign of Tess yet. Alison figured she wanted to make a grand entrance at the last minute. Main Street was strung across with flags and lined with spectators, sitting under sun hats and umbrellas. Alison fought back panic as she realized she would have to ride her bike past all these people.

Stop worrying, she told herself firmly. *You have a great chance of winning, and you're going to do your best!*

Alison took the number she was given and joined the other bicycles. She tried to sneak a glance at the other entries. As she had expected, they were mostly very ordinary—red, white, and blue paper streamers wrapped around handlebars. She could tell by the way the other kids looked at her that they thought hers was good. She proudly took her place in line.

After waiting in the hot sun for what seemed like hours, the marshal gave the whistle for the front of the parade to move off. The fire chief in his brightly polished antique fire truck started the parade, sirens blaring and bells ringing. From time to time the firemen would squirt the crowd with water from their hose. Alison could hear the screams and laughter up ahead as people were sprayed.

The high-school band struck up a song, horses' hooves clattered, and trucks with floats on them revved. Alison looked around for Tess. Maybe she hadn't been able to finish her bike after all. Maybe she had decided not to enter. *Maybe she wanted me to have a chance*, Alison thought, swiveling around in her seat to see the line of paper-wrapped bicycles behind her.

At the very last minute Tess appeared, red-faced and pedaling hard to get into line. Alison looked at the dragon and quickly looked again, unable to believe what she saw. The dragon wasn't very good. You could see the head had started off as a cardboard box and that the fire coming out of the mouth was just shiny red paper and cotton balls. The long tail that trailed behind the bike was stuck on with scotch tape and looked as if it had come off a couple of times on the way.

Poor Tess, Ali thought. But she couldn't also help feeling proud. For once, she had done something better than Tess, and even Tess would have to admire her. Then the bike in front of Alison started, and she was off.

It was not as hard as she had feared. The parade moved very slowly, stopping frequently.

Crowds cheered, people pointed at her and smiled, and she began to enjoy herself more and more. It was nice to be the person people looked at, the one getting the praise. As she neared the judges' stand, she saw her whole family. They started cheering loudly. "Yeah, Alison! Go, Ali! Great bike!" Ali blushed and giggled, trying to look straight ahead and concentrate on riding. She approached the stand and saw Mrs. Del Gado, wife of the police chief, walking toward her with a big blue rosette and an envelope.

"Congratulations, Alison, a charming effort," she said.

In a daze, Alison wheeled her bike to the police department parking lot where the parade officially ended. Strangers crowded around to congratulate her. Ali saw her family pushing through the crowd to get to her. She looked around and found Tess.

"I did it," Ali shouted, waving the envelope. "Look, Tess! Twenty-five dollars! We're going to have the greatest time."

Tess's face was bright red with anger. "Cheater!" she shouted, loud enough for everyone around to hear. "You cheated! You never built that bike yourself, Alison Hinkle."

Ali flushed, too, as people turned to stare. "You didn't have to," she said. "It didn't say in the rules you had to build it all yourself."

"But that's what it meant," Tess yelled. "It was for kids. Anyone could get grown-ups to do it for them and win!"

"I—I did most of it," Ali stammered. "My family just helped with the hard parts."

"Your family!" Tess shouted. "It's always your family! They do everything for you! They even win contests for you."

"They did not!" Ali shouted back. "I had the idea. I did most of it."

"I bet! You can't do anything without your mommie."

Ali's face was now the color of a radish. "Why do you always think you can make fun of me?" she yelled. "I don't make fun of you." Alison fought her hardest not to lose control. "Come on, Tess," she said. "What does it matter which of us won?"

"It matters to me!" Tess shouted. "Because I tried my hardest and I did it all myself. Nobody helped me."

"You're just jealous," Ali called as Tess started to wheel her bike away. "You can't stand it when anyone is better than you."

Tess turned back. "You can keep your dumb family," she yelled. "I never want to see any of you again."

She started to pedal away, her dragon's tail dragging in the dust.

Chapter 16

As Alison was congratulated and photographed, Tess's angry red face and cruel words buzzed around inside her head.

"I don't understand, Grandpa," she said afterward, as the old man fell into step beside her. "If she had won, I wouldn't have minded very much. I'd have been disappointed that it wasn't me, but I would have been glad it was her."

Her grandfather slipped a big, comforting arm around her shoulders. "Cheer up, punkin, we're all very proud of you."

"I thought she was my friend," Alison said bleakly. She got on her prize-winning bike and rode home, needing to be alone. She got home ahead of the others and went straight up to her room, shutting the door tightly behind her. She took off the frilly dress and put on her old shorts, trying hard not to cry. She sat on her bed and stared out the window.

Had Tess really meant what she said? she wondered. Would they both go home at the end of summer as if they had never been friends? Ali swallowed hard. At last she had known what it was like to have a best friend. It felt different than just being part of a group. Tess had come over just to see her in the mornings, she had slept over in her room, she had even saved her from the ghost. Now she and Tess wouldn't go to the carnival together or explore the octopus rock. She lay back and closed her eyes.

A while later, there was a light tap on her door and her mother came in the room carrying a tray.

"Grandma thought you might like a little snack," she said, putting it down on the bedside table. Ali didn't even look at it.

"The boys are going to the carnival in a little while," she said. "Why don't you get ready and go with them."

"I don't want to," Ali said, turning away.

"But you love the carnival," her mother said brightly. "You've looked forward to it all summer. Come on, cheer up and get dressed."

"I'm not going," Ali said.

"It will do you good," her mother said gently. "You'll have fun and forget all about the silly fight."

"It wasn't a silly fight," Ali said. "And I'm not going to the carnival."

"I really think . . . ," her mother began, but Ali sat up suddenly.

"Don't you understand?" she demanded. "I do not want to go to the carnival. Will you just leave me alone for once in my life?"

"Alison!" Mrs. Hinkle exclaimed. "I don't know what's gotten into you. I think maybe you're better off without Tess."

"Leave Tess out of this," Alison said, her voice wobbling on the edge of tears. "It's none of your business. Just go away. I want to be alone."

She turned her face toward the flowered wallpaper.

Her mother came over and patted her hair. "My Little Alligator," she said in a softer voice. "I know you're upset."

Ali turned back. "I'm not your Little Alligator anymore, Mom. I'm all grown up now, or I could be if you'd let me."

She rolled over and pulled the pillow over her head. Soon she heard her mother tiptoe from the room. She listened to the excited shouts of her brothers as they got ready to go to the carnival. They were really going without her. Ali couldn't believe it. She had stood up to her mother and won!

This should have been another victory to add to her twenty-five-dollar prize, but Ali didn't feel like celebrating. What good was anything if you didn't have a friend to share it with? She hoped Tess had gone to the carnival and seen that she wasn't there. Maybe then she'd realize that she had spoiled the thing Ali was most looking forward to. Maybe then she'd apologize.

After her family had left, Alison paced the empty house. She looked out the window and watched the sky fading from pink to gray. Suddenly she saw Tess, down on her hands and knees, crawling along the shrubbery. How strange Tess was! Why hadn't she just come right up to the door to say she was sorry? *Maybe she was creeping up to surprise me*, Ali decided. *Well, I'll surprise her instead.*

She slipped out the front door and around the side of the house. Then she came up behind Tess.

"Looking for something?" she demanded, hoping Tess would jump a mile and look guilty.

But Tess did not even look up. "Rajah," she said. "I can't find Rajah. I just thought he might have come over here."

"What happened?" Alison asked, dropping to her knees beside Tess.

Tess went on searching through the bushes. "I must not have closed his cage properly when I went out to the parade. When I got back, he was gone. I've been searching ever since."

"I'll help you look," Alison said.

"I've already looked just about everywhere," Tess said with a sigh. "All around the empty lot. I'm one giant scratch." She looked at the neatly kept lawns and flower beds that surrounded Ali's house. "I just thought this might be the kind of place he'd love . . . all the nice grass and flowers. I hoped he'd be here, but I don't think he is."

"He might be caught somewhere," Alison said. "You know, trapped in some wire or something?"

"That's what I was thinking," Tess agreed. "Or I'm sure he'd be home by now. Unless he's lost, that is."

They started moving through the garden, calling his name gently. Nothing stirred. The light was starting to fade. In the distance, dogs were barking excitedly. The girls paid no attention to the noise at first. Then, as the barking continued, the same thought began to form in both of their minds.

"You don't think . . . ," Alison started cautiously, because the thought was not a nice one.

"I was wondering exactly the same thing," Tess said in a panicked voice, jumping to her feet. "Come on!"

She ran like the wind in the direction of the barks, scrambling over the fence and across the empty lot, through brambles and bushes as if they didn't exist. Alison followed as fast as she could, but there was no way she could keep up. Tess's light, bouncing body moved farther and farther ahead, then vanished altogether as the noise of the barking grew louder. Alison heard shouts, a frightened yelp from a dog, then silence.

"Tess?" Alison called.

"Over here," came the faint voice.

"Have you found him?"

"Yes."

"Great," Alison said, plunging through the bushes.

She came upon Tess in a little hollow. Tess was crouched over a small brown shape.

"Is he okay?" Alison asked in a trembling voice, somehow knowing he wasn't.

Tess looked up. There was no expression in her dark eyes. "He's dead," she said.

Alison stood there feeling sick and awkward, not knowing what to say. For a long while Tess sat motionless, then she reached out to stroke the dead rabbit.

"It was my fault," she said, fighting to keep her voice calm. "I was in such a hurry to get to that parade. When I gave him his morning food, I didn't shut the cage properly." She spoke deliberately, as if she were a witness in court. "I bet he was trying to make friends with the wild rabbits. Look at all the rabbit holes around here. He went looking for friends . . . and then, when the dogs came, he wasn't smart enough to go down one of the holes. Maybe he was too fat. I fed him too well." She lifted a hand and wiped savagely at her eyes.

"I'll help you carry him home," Alison volunteered. "We can give him a nice funeral."

Tess got to her feet stiffly. "It's okay," she said. "He's not really heavy." The rabbit hung limply in her arms. "I'd rather be alone right now," she said. "Thanks for your help, though."

"You're welcome."

The two girls stood there looking at each other. There was so much Alison wanted to say. She wanted to tell Tess how sorry she was, that she understood what Tess was feeling. But Tess's face was so blank that she didn't say anything.

"I'll see you tomorrow, maybe," Alison said at last.

"Sure," Tess said. "I guess I won't be training for the circus anymore."

She started to plod away up the sandy slope. Alison watched her until she was just a black silhouette against the fading light.

Chapter 17

In the middle of the night Alison lay awake, her heart aching for Tess and Rajah. Tess didn't have a big, loving family like Ali's, just a strange, moody father and a mother who was far away. Rajah had been really important to her.

If only there was something I could do, Alison thought, tossing and turning in her bed. Then slowly an idea began to form in her head. It was a brilliant, beautiful idea. She was so excited that she wanted to tell Tess about it right away. Then she decided it would be much better to surprise Tess.

The next morning, Alison cornered Grandpa as soon as he got up. "I need to go into town this morning," she said. "Can you drive me? Please?"

Grandpa looked at her curiously. "Meeting with a secret admirer?" he asked.

"Nothing like that," she said. She looked around. "Promise you won't tell?"

"Cross my heart," Grandpa said.

"Tess's rabbit died," Alison said. "I'm going to

use the twenty-five dollars I won to get her a new rabbit. They have lop-eared rabbits at the pet shop, and I know Tess likes those best."

"We'll go right after my walk," Grandpa said. "We'll be there when the stores open."

"Thanks, Grandpa," Alison said.

Grandpa patted her hand. "Tess is lucky to have a friend like you."

Alison could hardly sit still on the way to the store. The saleswoman helped her select a beautiful baby lop-eared rabbit. "You need a young one if you really want to train it," she said. "This one is a real sweetie pie."

"He's perfect," Alison said. "I know Tess will love him." She clutched the box all the way home in the car, peering in through the air holes every two minutes to make sure the rabbit hadn't vanished.

"Would you drive me straight to Tess's house, Grandpa?" she asked. "I can't wait any longer."

Grandpa smiled and pulled into Tess's driveway.

Max opened the door. He studied Alison and the box for a moment, then said, "She might not want to see you. She hasn't gotten out of bed since yesterday afternoon."

"I'll go up anyway," Alison said. She was so excited that she wasn't even intimidated by Max. She pushed past him and went up the stairs. She knocked, then went in without waiting for an answer. Tess was lying among the stuffed animals, her arms wrapped tightly around her big green dinosaur.

"Hi," Alison said.

"I don't want to talk right now, okay?" Tess said, her voice muffled by the dinosaur. "I'm not feeling too good."

"I've brought you something that will make you feel better," Alison said. She walked toward Tess and presented her with the box.

"What is it?" Tess asked, sitting up cautiously.

"Open it and see."

Slowly, Tess let go of the dinosaur. Then she opened the lid of the box. She let out a gasp. "It's a rabbit."

"It's for you," Alison said. "It's a new rabbit. Now you can go on with your circus training."

During her ride back from town, Alison had imagined this moment several times. She imagined that Tess would jump up, throw her arms around Ali, and tell her she was the best friend in the whole world. But now, as she looked at Tess's face, Ali knew that was not going to happen. Tess's face was not full of joy, as Ali had pictured, but flushed and angry. She scrambled up from her bed and backed away as if the box contained a rattlesnake. "Take it away," she yelled. "I don't want it. You can't just replace something you loved!"

"B-b-but, Tess," Alison stammered. "I know he can't replace Rajah, but he's very sweet and he might make you feel better."

"How would you know what would make me feel better?" Tess shouted. "You have no idea, you and your stupid family. You've probably never lost anything in your entire life! Everybody loves you and takes care of you." She pushed the box toward Alison. "Take it away," she said. "I don't want it." "I don't need anything or anyone!"

As Ali stared at the box in front of her, her own anger spilled over. "It's a good thing you're not going to keep him," she shouted. "You'd better stick to your stupid stuffed animals, because you don't know how to treat living things. I'll just take him back to the pet store. They'll find him a good home with a person who knows how to love him, a person who knows how to have friends, because you sure don't."

She scooped up the box, holding it close to her. "I used my prize money, my own twenty-five dollars, to buy this for you," she said. "Even after all the horrible things you said to me, I still wanted to make you happy. But you're just a spoiled brat."

"Spoiled? Me?" Tess screamed.

"Sure you're spoiled," Alison said. "Your parents let you do whatever you want. You always get your own way. That's why you couldn't take it when you didn't win the contest."

"I couldn't take it because the winner only won with lots of help, and it wasn't fair."

"That's not true," Alison said. "I only had a little help. I spent hours working on it."

"But I did mine all by myself," Tess said. "I had nobody to help me." Her voice dropped. "I never do."

"Just because your parents let you be independent . . . ," Alison began, but Tess cut in.

"Parent," she said. "Parent in the singular. I only have one. Maggie's gone."

"But she'll be back soon."

"No, she won't," Tess said. She looked up defiantly and met Alison's gaze. "She left. She's not coming back. She wants to be alone."

Alison didn't know what to say. How could Tess have kept this to herself all this time?

"Maggie only wanted to come to the beach to see if she and Max could patch things up," Tess went on. "Things have been bad for a while. As soon as we got here, she realized it was no good. So she left." She brushed away a tear. "I helped her pack," she said. "I thought she might change her mind." Another tear escaped, running all the way down Tess's cheek to her chin.

"Maybe she'll have you come as soon as she's settled," Alison suggested. "Maybe you could go to school in Florida. I hear it's really nice there. You could visit Disneyworld."

Tess shook her head. "She doesn't want me."

"Of course she wants you," Alison said, shocked. "She's your mother."

Tess shook her head even harder. "She said she loves me, but she wants to be alone for a while to sort things out. She says I'm better off with Max in the city."

Her voice wavered. Alison put the box down. "I'm sorry, Tess," she said. "I had no idea."

"I didn't want you to know," Tess said. "I didn't think you'd understand. . . . Not with a family like yours."

She paused and kicked the stuffed animals, sending them tumbling onto the floor. "That's why I felt so bad when you won the parade," she said. "You had your family to help you. It seemed so unfair that you should have people to love you and help you win contests, too."

"I only asked them to help because I thought I wasn't good enough on my own," Alison said. "I was sure your entry would be great and mine would be boring. But I would have been really happy if you'd won."

Tess looked away. "I guess I'm just not a nice

person," she said at last. "Would you please go away now? I hate for anybody to see me cry."

Tess had already curled up again and turned her back to Alison. Alison thought she might cry, too. She quickly picked up the box, tiptoed down the stairs, and ran out the front door all the way home.

Chapter 18

Alison sat alone on the octopus rock and trailed her hand in the water. She had carried the rabbit home and gone straight out again. She needed to be alone to put her confused thoughts in order. She had walked and walked, wandering aimlessly until finally she had picked her way out to the rock. Now she peered down into the green depths, watching anemones and seaweed swaying in the marine forest below her.

Poor Tess, she thought, *after all that she has been through, no wonder she acts mean.* But she still couldn't squash the angry, hurt thoughts inside her head. *She didn't even trust me enough to share her problems with me,* Ali thought. *I guess we weren't best friends after all.*

Now, as Ali thought about it, she realized that Tess had told her almost nothing about herself. Ali had told Tess about her friends and her life at school, about how unimportant it sometimes felt to be in between two brothers, about how her mother babied her—and Tess had told her nothing! Ali realized she knew nothing about Tess's friends or her life in New York. She could have forgiven Tess for not talking about those things. But not telling her friend that her mother had left—that was something Ali found hard to forgive.

She was so deep in thought that she didn't hear the sound of soft footsteps over the seaweed. When Tess spoke, Ali almost fell into the water.

"Are you looking for the octopus?" Tess asked.

"Not really."

"Do you think he's still there?"

"Who knows?"

There was a long silence. A wave rushed in and slapped against the rocks.

"I was looking all over for you," Tess said at last. "I just wanted to ask you . . . um . . . if you'd taken the rabbit back to the store."

"Not yet," Alison said. "It's at my house. I didn't want to ask Grandpa to drive me back again."

"I think I've changed my mind," Tess said at last. "It would be a shame to take it back to the pet store when I've got a good cage with nothing in it. Would you mind if I kept it after all?"

"Whatever," Alison said, shrugging her shoulders.

"Ali?" Tess asked in a small voice. "Are you mad at me?"

"Yes."

"Because I didn't want the rabbit when you were nice enough to get it for me?"

"No, not because of that."

"What, then?"

"Because I thought you were my friend," Ali said in a strangled voice.

"I am."

"No, you're not," Alison said, looking up angrily. "Friends don't keep secrets from each other. You didn't even trust me enough to tell me your mother had left."

"I couldn't," Tess said. "It hurt too much to talk about it."

"It might have helped to share it," Alison said.

Tess shook her head. "I'm not used to sharing," she said. "I'm not good at it."

"What about your friends at school—don't you tell them things?" Alison asked.

Tess shook her head again. "I don't have any friends at school," she said. "They always move me around before I have a chance to make friends. Every time I got settled in a school, Max and Maggie would hear about another one that sounded better. I've already been to five schools."

Alison stared into the green depths, considering this. She had started with the same friends in kindergarten. She couldn't imagine what it would be like to go to a school where you knew nobody.

Even at the big junior high, she would still have all her old classmates.

"You're the first real friend I've ever had," Tess said. "You stuck by me, even after I said horrible things to you. You bought me the rabbit. . . . I guess I don't blame you if you don't want to be friends anymore."

"I do want to be friends," Alison said slowly, "if you do."

"I do," Tess answered. "I really do."

"You want to start over?" Alison asked at last.

Tess nodded. "Only, I might need some help. I'm not very good at it, I guess." She knelt beside Ali and stared down into the water.

"Sometimes you are," Alison said. "I've never had as much fun with anyone else. It's been a great summer. I'd never have done all those crazy things without you."

"Okay, then," Tess said, as if the matter was settled. She trailed her hand into the water, then jerked it back. "Ali!" she yelled. "I saw it! The octopus—I saw it down there! Ohmygosh, it was huge! Do you think it's the kind that will reach up and grab us?"

"No way," Ali said, laughing nervously. "Octopi are supposed to be shy."

Tess's eyes lit up. "Hey, what a great title for a song: 'Octopi Are Supposed to Be Shy'!" she shouted. "I've got to tell my dad. Maybe it'll be a hit and we'll get rich."

"Octopi are supposed to be shy! Octopi are supposed to be shy!" she sang.

She started to do a funky dance, stepped on a patch of wet seaweed, flailed her arms wildly, and fell into the water. Ali started to laugh. Tess came to the surface and grabbed at the rocks.

"Don't just stand there, get me out of here!" she yelled. "There's a monster octopus down there. It will get me."

"It's supposed to be shy," Ali said, laughing helplessly as she offered her hand to Tess.

"I'm not so sure about that," Tess shouted, dragging herself up the steep rock with Ali's help. "I think it might be . . ." She stopped, opened her eyes wide, and let out a yell. "It's got me! Ali, help, it's got me!"

Alison peered down. "It's only seaweed," she said, yanking Tess up onto dry land. "You had seaweed wrapped around your leg."

"No kidding?" Tess asked, gasping for breath. "I was sure it had me." She pushed her hair back from her face. "Thanks," she said. "You saved me from the seaweed."

"That's what friends are for," Alison said, looking at her seriously. "You can count on them. They won't let you down."

Tess nodded and got slowly to her feet. "I'd better go change these clothes," she said quietly.

"You can come back to my house and borrow some," Ali said.

"Thanks," Tess said. Then she paused. "Maybe we could get the rabbit at the same time."

"Sure," Alison said. They started to pick their way back over the rocks.

"You want to go to the carnival tonight?" Ali asked.

"Definitely!"

"We'll only be able to go on a few rides, though. I spent all my prize money on the rabbit."

"That's okay. We'll just go on the best ones. Maybe Max will give me a few extra dollars, because I was so sad about my rabbit."

"And maybe my family will give me extra, because I was so sad about you."

They looked at each other and smiled.

"I guess families do have their uses," Tess said.

"I guess so," Ali agreed.

As she was changing for the carnival that evening, her mother knocked on her door. This time she waited for Ali to call, "Come in."

"I'm glad you're going to the carnival," she said. "It would have been a shame to miss it. I hear you and Tess have made up."

Ali nodded.

Her mother perched on the end of her bed. "I hope she apologized."

"It's okay. I understand now," Ali said. "You know how we thought her mother was at an art show? Well, she's not. She's left them and gone to live on her own."

Ali's mother looked horrified. "Poor little girl." She shook her head. "Imagine a mother walking out on her family."

"There are times when I wish you'd walk out on us," Ali said with a grin.

"Ali, that's a terrible thing to say," her mother said, but she smiled. "I suppose I am a pain sometimes."

"Sometimes," Ali said, looking at her fondly.

Mrs. Hinkle looked down and ran her finger along the crease in Ali's comforter. "It's hard for mothers to let go. They want to protect their children from anything that could hurt them."

"I know that, Mom," Ali said, "but you have to let me grow up. I'm almost a teenager now."

There was silence in the room. Ali's mother nodded as if she were thinking. Then she looked up suddenly. "Are you too grown up to give your mother a hug?"

"I guess not," Ali said. "Not this year, anyway."

She walked over to her mother and wrapped her arms around her tightly.

On the last night of the carnival, Ali and Tess sat together high on the Ferris wheel, looking down at the sea of lights and listening to the music from the merry-go-rounds, the squeals from the Gravitron riders, and the shouts from the midway. Taking up more than his fair share of the seat was a giant stuffed unicorn.

"Wasn't it nice of Josh's friend to let you have a fourth ball free?" Tess asked.

"I still can't believe I won this," Ali said, wrapping her arms around its neck.

"Now you can start your own stuffed-animal collection," Tess said. "He's more beautiful than any of mine. Don't tell my dinosaur I said that, though."

"I want you to have him," Ali said.

"Ali! No way. You won him,"

"I know, but you really wanted him," Ali said. "I'm giving him to you on one condition."

"What?"

"That you bring him back next summer," Ali said. "That way I know I'll see you again."

"Of course you'll see me again, you goob," Tess said. "I'll keep on bugging Max until he agrees to come back here." She looked at Ali and smiled. "Now that I've found a person who can put up with me, you don't think I'm going to let you get away, do you?"

The Ferris wheel started moving again, bringing them down toward the noise and the lights. The smell of french fries and cotton candy rose to meet them. Their seat came to rest at the bottom. Tess released the bar and jumped out. "Come on, Ali," she yelled. "Hot dogs or Gravitron?" Then she was off, moving over the trampled grass as if she had springs in her feet.

Here's a sneak preview of what happens when Jasmine, Tess's glamorous fourteen-year-old friend from California, comes to Rose Bay for the summer in FRIENDS #2:

Tess & Ali and the Teeny Bikini

They were crossing the bridge to the island when Jasmine said to Peter, "I really like this car. It moves so well."

Peter looked pleased. "I do a lot of work on it," he said. "Want to drive?"

"Sure," Jasmine said.

Ali opened her mouth to say that Jasmine didn't have a license yet, but Tess nudged her. "She drives fine," Tess whispered. "I've driven with her. Besides, it's totally deserted out here. Don't worry."

Jasmine was already in the driver's seat. She clicked her seatbelt shut and released the brake. The car moved forward smoothly. Ali gradually started breathing again. Jasmine did seem to know how to drive after all, and Tess was right—

the road was deserted at this time of day. As Jasmine picked up confidence, she started to drive faster.

"Wow, this car is awesome. I want one just like it," she shouted to Peter.

"Don't miss the turn to Rose Bay," Ali warned.

The turn came up on the left, almost hidden behind a row of pine trees. Jasmine saw it at the last minute and braked hard. The next moment the wheels were sliding over the sandy surface. Jasmine screamed. Ali was frozen. Peter tried to grab the wheel.

"Steer into the skid!" he was yelling.

The world seemed to be spinning around and around in slow motion. Ali grabbed Tess and closed her eyes, waiting for the final, inevitable crash.

Suddenly she realized they weren't spinning any more. She opened her eyes. The car had come to rest beside the road, among blueberry bushes and tall ferns. Everyone breathed again.

"Phew, that was lucky," Peter said.

"I'm sorry," Jasmine muttered. "I didn't see the stupid turn until it was too late."

"It's okay. It wasn't your fault. There's a lot of sand on the road," Peter said. "Let's just hope we can get out of this field."

"I hope I haven't scratched your car," Jasmine said.

"Don't worry about it," Peter said. "Maybe I'd better drive the rest of the way." He got out of the car. "No real damage done," he called as he climbed into the driver's seat. Very gently he eased the car, wheels protesting against the scrub and sand, back onto the road. A few minutes later, they pulled up outside Ali's house and the three girls got out.

Jasmine waved and called to Peter, "Bye, see you tomorrow," as if nothing had happened. Tess waved, too, and Peter drove off.

Ali's legs were trembling so much they would hardly obey her. She grabbed Tess and pulled her aside. "I hope you're satisfied," she said. "Jasmine nearly got us killed!"

Tess shook her off. "Don't make such a big thing out of it. We're okay, aren't we? Nothing really happened."

"Nothing really happened?" Ali shouted. "She was risking our lives."

"Ali, it was just a little skid," Tess said. "And we're fine. So forget about it. I'm sure Peter won't let her drive again. There's nothing to worry about."

"Oh, sure," Ali muttered. "Do you know what my parents would say if they heard about this?"

Tess glanced at Jasmine, who was leaning

against the gate post looking bored. She winced as if she was embarrassed by Ali's outburst. "Come on, Al," Tess whispered. "Calm down, okay?"

"You want me to calm down?" Ali shouted. "Oh, I'm just so uncool because I don't pretend I'm eighteen and crash cars."

Tess glanced at Jasmine again. Jasmine was examining her fingernails.

"What's the matter with you this summer? You're no fun anymore," Tess said. "You're either worrying or sulking."

"No fun anymore?" Ali shouted even louder now. "Is that your idea of fun—nearly flipping over in a car?"

"It didn't nearly flip over. It turned around a couple of times," Tess said, shrugging her shoulders and sticking her hands into the pockets of her shorts.

"Come on, Tess, I want to get home and take a shower," Jasmine called impatiently.

Ali longed to take Tess and shake her. *Stop acting like this! Stop pretending you're Jasmine and be the way you really are*, she wanted to shout. But she knew it was useless.

"Okay," Ali said in what she hoped was a calm voice. "Maybe I'm just immature, but I don't want to hang around Jasmine anymore. I guess you can't be friends with both of us."

Tess opened her mouth in surprise. "Hey, Al, you don't mean that, do you?"

"Sure, I do."

Tess hesitated. Ali could see her trying to decide what to do next. She drew in the sand with her toes. "Look, Al, she's my guest," Tess said.

"Fine," Ali said, and she heard her voice quiver. "But I'm through tagging along with the two of you."

She turned and hurried into the house before she started to cry.

Enter the FRIENDS Phone Giveaway and Ultimate Pen Pal Match-up!

WIN A PAIR OF PHONES!
One for you, one for your friend

100 Grand Prizes— The first 100 respondents receive a pair of FRIENDS phones

500 First Prizes— The next 500 respondents win *Homecoming*, Book #1 in Janet Quin-Harkin's SENIOR YEAR series, coming in October 1991 from HarperPaperbacks

EVERYONE GETS A FRIENDS PEN PAL!

All you have to do is follow the instructions below.
All entries must be returned by October 30, 1991.

Official Rules:

1. No purchase necessary to win. You can enter by completing the Official Coupons in each of the four books in the HarperPaperbacks FRIENDS series and sending all four coupons together to:

    FRIENDS PHONE GIVEAWAY
    HarperPaperbacks
    10 East 53rd Street
    16th Floor
    New York, NY 10022
    DEPT: LB

You can also enter by copying each of the four coupons exactly on separate 3 x 5 cards and sending all four together to the address above.

2. Entries must be postmarked by October 30, 1991. Prizes will be awarded as follows: Pair of phones—first 100 complete entries received; Book #1, SENIOR YEAR—101st-600th complete entries received; pen pals—all respondents who request one. No prize substitution, mechanically reproduced entries, or transfers allowed. HarperPaperbacks is not responsible for incomplete or lost or misdirected entries. In the event of a tie in receipt of entries, winners will be picked at random.

3. Prize winners and their parents may be required to execute an Affidavit of Eligibility and Promotional Release supplied by HarperPaperbacks. Entering the Giveaway constitutes permission for use of winners' names, addresses, and likenesses for publicity and promotional purposes, with no additional compensation.

4. Employees of HarperCollins Publishers, Inc., its affiliates, and their immediate family members are not eligible for this Giveaway. This Giveaway is open only to residents of the United States and Canada (void in Quebec) aged 18 or younger. Void where prohibited or restricted by law. All federal, state, and local regulations apply. Taxes, if any, are the winner's sole responsibility.

5. For a list of Grand Prize winners, send a stamped, self-addressed envelope, entirely separate from your entry, to FRIENDS PHONE GIVEAWAY, HarperPaperbacks, 10 East 53rd Street, 16th floor, New York, NY 10022, DEPT: LB

FRIENDS PHONE GIVEAWAY
Official Coupon Book #1, *Starring Tess & Ali*

Name _____ Age _____
Address _____
City _____ State _____ Zip _____
_____ I would like to be matched with a FRIENDS pen pal.
(If you do not request one, you will *not* be matched with a pen pal.)

Where did you get this FRIENDS book?

_____ Bookstore   _____ Drugstore   _____ Supermarket
_____ Book Club   _____ Book Fair   _____ Library   _____ Other